SMALL BRUTAL INCIDENTS

MICHAEL DITTMAN

contemporary press

This is a work of fiction. All of the characters and events portrayed in this book are either products of the author's twisted imagination or are used fictitiously.

Small Brutal Incidents

Cover design by Chris Reese
Cover photograph by Chris Reese

A Contemporary Press Book
Published by Contemporary Press
Brooklyn, New York

Distributed by Publishers Group West
www.pgw.com

www.contemporarypress.com

ISBN 0-9766579-2-9

First Edition: June 2006

Printed in the United States of America

SMALL BRUTAL INCIDENTS

MICHAEL DITTMAN

Liner Notes

The author wishes to thank his family, especially Amy and Helen.

In addition, this book would not have been possible without the careful editing and encouragement of Jess Dukes.

My idiosyncratic version of Pittsburgh would not have been possible without the inspiration of the books of Michael Chabon and Tom Lipinski; the photography of Tim Fabian and W. Eugene Smith; the films of Rick Sebak and George Romero; and the exhibits of the Senator John Heinz Pittsburgh Regional History Center.

My gratitude to you all.

1

[handwritten annotation: Not in 1946 C.P., 5? Try Carnegie'12 Tech!]

It was a strange thing and a difficult one to understand, but it started in the pool at <u>Carnegie Mellon University</u>. Blood languidly oozed out of the naked body of a young man. There was a round, puckered flower of a puncture wound on the smooth skin of his back, blossoming just under and slightly to the right of his left shoulder blade. If he were to have rolled over like a ship in a heavy storm, the other exit wound would have been visible in his chest, a hole large enough for a pinkie finger to penetrate without touching the ragged sides of the opening. If he had listed over, the cops stalking around the pool trying to find the best angle to get a hold of his body would have seen the look of shock on this face, a look that would have disturbed their sleep; a look that they would have tried to drink or screw away, all the while just scratching it deeper into their mind. Instead, they made jokes about slipping on the wet tile, and smirked at each other about the deep scratches on the dead guy's buttocks as they became clearly visible along with the pink blood that rose to the surface from between them.

They chased him around the pool as if they were bobbing for apples. Finally, when the coroner's assistant slipped a lifeguard's rescue hook around the boy's shoulders, the body weakly accepted and drifted towards the gutter. In the silence, the water lapped and exhaled nosily, sucking its way down vented slots in the gutter. It took three cops to haul him out and lay him face up on the cool tile. An older wound on his forehead wrinkled where the scab had fallen off from its soaking. Blood dripped from his body across the tile in tiny red rivers, then landed in the gutter and disappeared, only to re-enter the pool moments later from the recirculation vents. Sunlight drifted through soot-encrusted skylights and reflected off the water, giving the whole room a carnival funhouse vibe. The light dappled and played tricks. It disrupted the policemen's sense of distance and several times, some of them found themselves stepping forward where they thought there was solid ground only to find nothing. The pool's bleachers climbed up the sides of the building and at the top, where the windows hung, their eyes were blinded so that the seats seemed to climb forever. The light off the top of the water dazzled, and along with the smell of blood and chlorine, they tasted a sourness at the back of their necks.

But the ravaged body bothered no one. It was so utterly alien, so inhuman in his pale nakedness that no one thought to get sick, not even the younger cops. They stared transfixed at his shrunken genitals, his cloudy eyes. And then, they thought about what they would eat for lunch, when they would next get laid. They even took up joking among themselves again, until one of the cops found a silver bracelet behind the bleachers.

"Oh shit," he said. "Detective?"

Detective Sharp was still a young man, and still had his looks. He had what he had considered, up to this point, a good life. He was unmarried and liked to drink, liked women, liked his job. He was thinking about the girl he had met last night, when McClusky, the young patrolman, just transferred from Braddock, called him.

"Yeah?"

"You better see this."

Sharp picked up the bracelet. It was too dainty, too easily torn or broken by work to be worn by most men, yet it was still heavier, chunkier than what a woman would wear. Across the plate in cursive engraving read, *Ketchum*.

"Fuck," said Detective Sharp. "I thought he looked familiar."

They all gathered around the corpse of Stephen Ketchum, looking at the bracelet and then back at the boy, no more than 19 or 20, slim and thin-lipped with copper hair cut close to the scalp, and his body hairless except for the shock around his genitals.

"Body's been dead for a while. He's already been hard, now he's all limp again. Looks like he got an unexpected delivery in the rear," said Mooney, the coroner, to one of his white-coated assistants and anyone else listening. Turning to the detective, he asked, "Are you done here?" Mooney had started to sweat in the damp heat of the building. The pool was heated by coal-fired furnaces which filled the room with the wet heat of a greenhouse. Under Mooney's overcoat, the fat man's shirt was already soaked through. He pushed his hair back from his forehead and mopped the sweat from his brow.

"Oh yes," said Sharp, "Jesus, but we are done."

The same three cops who had hauled the body out of the pool rolled it into an olive green body bag that crinkled in the humidity, a sound that danced around the high-ceilinged pool room. They zipped it, tossed it without ceremony onto a gurney, and wheeled it out to the waiting car.

Detective Sharp dropped the bracelet in his pocket and walked over to the coroner.

"Is he who I think he is?" asked Mooney.

"Yep."

"You have to tell his old man?"

"Not until I get a full report from you."

"But you'll be the one to tell him?"

"Yep."

"Better you than me," said Sharp, walking away.

To save money, the maintenance staff didn't drain the pool. Instead, they closed it for two days and shocked it with chlorine. The blood was caught in the filters and the chlorine bleached it out until only the grout between the tile kept its pink—and even that was gone within a week.

2

Or at least that's what I was told, much, much later. The fall of 1946 was an awkward one. The days didn't seem to get any shorter as the months unraveled. Instead, the slanted fall light still lasted into the evenings, fooling people into happiness. People drank too much, kissed their neighbor's wives in the dark recesses of parties where the steaks weren't even put on the grill until almost ten o'clock, and by the time they were done everyone was too drunk to stop to eat. Strings of lights blotted out the fall stars and the harvest moon. Cars leaked gasoline stink in the driveways, shutting out the warm smell of acorns. Cigarette smoke wrestled the leaf-burning fires of suburbia to the dirt and immobilized them, slithering through keyholes and filling the homes of the most dedicated non-smokers, tickling the upstairs noses of children who dozed lightly as the sound of the parties drifted up from new patios.

Except in my home. Here, tension prevailed. Elizabeth, my daughter, went upstairs earlier than her bedtime required. She disappeared no later than 7 p.m. while there were still snatches of light peeking around curtains that did nothing to deaden the sounds of the other neighborhood children playing around the legs of their parents, dizzy with unbridled freedom and the innocence of the strangeness of this fall. Elizabeth slept, I think now, to avoid the fight that always seemed ready to break out between her mother and me. I hadn't worked in six months, which seemed unthinkable to everyone around us, including Mary's parents. It would have been an easy thing for any guy to walk down to the mill, and be hired to sweep floors the next day ... if that guy wasn't me. I was blackballed from working not just at these furnaces, but the ones in Homestead too, even as far north as New Castle and Youngstown. At any furnace that was related to Carnegie or Mellon, they had my name memorized as a rabble-rouser, an instigator, and probably a Communist. So, I slept in while Mary got Lizzie ready for school. Mary went to work around nine in the morning four days a week clerking at Woolworth's. I got dressed around ten, after Mary and Lizzie and the men of the neighborhood left and a silence filtered over the lawns like a narcotic fog, and then sat in the house.

And nothing ever happened. That's why it's easy to remember Wednesday, September 14. That was the morning the doorbell rang and a well-dressed man asked for me by name.

For some people marriage is a callous, where their true self is hidden beneath a hardened layer of skin absorbing all the blows of day-to-day life. For Mary, marriage was like the disease that attacks trees, gnawing away their heartwood until they're empty inside, and you never know if the next strong wind will bring them toppling down, maybe to crush you. For me, marriage was the hard pressure of the Earth that turns a worthless piece of coal into a diamond, waiting to be split and set, waiting for a moment like the ringing of my doorbell.

"I can't go," I said to the man at the door. He was tall and heavy-set. He missed a place shaving about the size a pencil eraser, and I found myself talking to these bristly hairs rather than meeting his eyes, red-rimmed and hollow.

"My wife won't know where I am."

"Leave her a note, jackass."

"Where would I tell her I'm going?"

"Out," he said.

"I'm busy. Another time, maybe." And I started to shut the door. His wingtip shot between the sill and the door. Careless, I thought. That shoe had to cost more than ten steak dinners.

"Your schedule cleared when Mrs. Ketchum wanted talk to you."

"Ketchum? What's she want?" I knew the name, only not with the "Mrs." attached. Ketchum ran things at the mill where I had worked. His was the name that had showed up on both my check and my pink slip.

"You'll find out when we get there."

"But ..."

He shot his face closer to the sill, his mouth suddenly congenial. I smelled his breath. Anise, I thought. He had sausage for breakfast.

"Listen jackass, do you think anyone will care if I beat the living shit out of you right here in your own front yard? Personally, I think they'd be so glad to see the neighborhood pinko get his nuts ripped off that they would line the streets and cheer."

So I went with him, against my better judgment. And I didn't leave a note. His car was cool inside and he smoked deeply on a Lucky Strike, which I secretly wanted. He wasn't as fat as I remembered the mill security guys to be, guys too stupid to be Pinkertons picked up in local lunch counters and bars for piecework. Mill muscle like that worked just for the privilege to drive around in long black Lincoln and beat people up. The money was pure gravy. This guy seemed to have a little class in his dress and demeanor, although his mouth ran like a duck's ass.

"To tell you the truth, I don't know what Mrs. Ketchum wants with a load like you. Maybe she needs someone to clean up after her dog. All I know is she gives me your name and address and when I saw you I recognized you, which made the chance of beating the living shit out of you all the sweeter."

The streets were lined with the first falling leaves. They swirled behind us, and a squirrel ran in the street. The sun felt good on my face. I realized it had been weeks since I had last felt it. I closed my eyes and enjoyed the smell of the smoke and the warm light across my face. We slowed and then accelerated again hypnotically. When the well-dressed muscle finished his smoke, he flicked the butt out the window and popped a Sen-Sen. Anise, I thought, of course.

"Wakey-wakey, we're here."

The driveway curved around to the house. A big one. The kind that when I was a kid, my dad would drive us around to look at their Christmas lights before we headed back to our dark home. We pulled to the front and when I reached for the door, I was told to wait in the car.

I watched as he went to the door and rang the bell. The door opened slowly, words were exchanged, and then he motioned for me to come up. It was a million dollar house in a million dollar neighborhood. I couldn't even afford to take out the garbage here. Inside, everything was cool and polished, and my run-down heels clicked off the gleaming wood floor as I followed the driver to a set of pocket doors. He opened them a sliver.

"Mrs. Ketchum?" he asked quietly and then turned to me. "Don't do anything stupid jackass, I'll be right outside."

It was easy to see that she has been pretty, even beautiful, once. Mrs. Ketchum was a small woman, with her hair bobbed around her neck, a style from an older time. She was forty-five, fifty maybe, but wore the dress of a younger woman and had the legs to match. She walked to the bar cart and poured herself a drink. After slugging it down, she said, "Sit down," with her back to me. There was the shivering hiss of a desk lighter and when she turned around, she held a brown cigarette between her fingers.

"Cigarette, Mr. Burns?"

"Yes, please."

She took another brown cigarette out of an ornate box and after handing it to me, passed me the lighter. It was an airplane. Older and heavy, pure silver. I hadn't seen anything like it, even for sale, for probably fifteen years, pre-war. As I took the lighter from her, I noticed that my hands were shaking, but hers weren't. The smoke hissed through me, washing calm into my brain. Cigarettes were a luxury for me since I had stopped working. Mary didn't mind giving it up, but it was hell for me.

"Do you know who I am, Mr. Burns?"

"Sure. Felice Ketchum. Wife of John Ketchum, the man who used to sign my checks."

"'Used to' being the operative words, yes."

"That's right, I don't work for your husband anymore."

She laughed a little and smoke curled out of the nose. "You never worked for my husband, Mr. Burns. The money, the company, all belongs to me and my family. He simply married it. His name may be on the checks, but it comes from my vault."

"Either way, it doesn't worry me anymore. The Ketchum name isn't on my checks anymore."

"As I understand it, you don't have any checks for names to appear. Times have been rough for you lately, hmm?"

I shrugged, "It's been better."

"I'm sure," she said. "Does your wife enjoy working?"

"She doesn't mind," I lied.

"Woolworth's? Must be difficult seeing the neighbor ladies come in, having to ring up friend's purchases. The brutal thing being that even these small incidentals, these five-and-dime purchases, are small purchases that your wife couldn't possibly afford."

"Mrs. Ketchum ..."

"And all the gossip of course. The shame of the in-laws. Must be dreadful. Let me ask you this, did you enjoy working for me, Mr. Burns?"

"I enjoyed the people I met."

"Do you feel that I treated you fairly?"

"I don't think any owners treat their workers fairly."

She smiled. "You're a romantic one aren't you, Mr. Burns?" For a moment, I saw the beauty that she once was and my heart skipped a beat. She walked close to me, then behind me, which I felt.

"My son, Stephen, was a romantic as well." She paused and took a deep drag. "He was a beautiful boy—blond curls and light blue eyes. I loved him. When he was a boy, I loved dressing him up in tiny little white outfits. Because of the soot of this damned city, I would change his clothes, three or four times a day. I gave him everything he wanted—cars, horses, houses, trips. He had soft hands. Beautiful, soft hands. Let me see your hands Mr. Burns." I held out my hands palm down. They were shaking again as she moved to the front of the chair.

"Turn them over."

My hands were still yellow with calluses, but they weren't swollen with work. "Yours are getting soft, aren't they Mr. Burns?"

"Not really."

"You're the sort of man who needs to work, aren't you, Mr. Burns?" I sat silently, and then realized my hands still hung extended. I pulled them in.

"Not like my husband. He's perfectly happy to leave the office after an hour in the morning, and spend the rest of the day golfing or lunching."

"I don't mind hard work."

"That's what I understand. You were a Marine weren't you, Graeme?"

"Yes ma'am." The woman scared me, not just because she knew everything about me, but also because she treated my life story as if it were common information, as if I were as much a part of her day as the weather.

"Pacific Theater, I seem to remember."

"Yes, the Tarawas and Peleliu."

"A nasty one."

"Yes, ma'am."

"And you killed men."

"Yes ma'am."

"What did it feel like?"

"Work ma'am. It felt like hard, dirty work."

"My son was killed two nights ago. I'm off to bury him after I'm done with you."

"I'm sorry, Mrs. Ketchum."

"So am I, Mr. Burns. So am I."

I had seen Stephen around the mill in summers. An only child, he went to Carnegie Mellon. He spent his workdays walking around aimlessly in the plant, wandering into dangerous areas until other people screamed at him. Several times we saw his father, in business suit and hardhat, dress him down on the floor, screaming at him in front of everyone. When they left, workers talked about how Mr. Ketchum was no different than any hillbilly pig who lived deep in the woods around Kittanning.

There was a pause in her interrogation as she walked over to the bar cart and fixed herself another drink. When she turned around, her face was pinched hard and tight around her eyes.

"Would you like to work again, Mr. Burns?" It wasn't meant as a question, and I tried not to answer. I started sweating through my shirt, which was already gray from the soot in the Pittsburgh air. I didn't want to be here anymore. I wanted to be back in that big car, with the sun warm on my face, not knowing where I was headed.

"It would depend on the type of work I guess."

"What if I said I could take you off the blacklist? You could find work wherever you wanted. Work in the mill again, make a good living. Mary could quit her job."

"I don't know if I want to go back to the mill, thank you very much, Mrs. Ketchum."

"What if I hired you off the books? For $10,000. And got your name off the list."

"I'm not sure I understand, Mrs. Ketchum," but I was afraid I did.

"The police will never find my son's killer. Oh, they'll find someone. Already they've found a Negro and they're calling his death a botched robbery, but my son was killed in a peculiarly brutal way that, to me, doesn't suggest robbery."

"Why not get Mr. Ketchum ..."

She waved her hand. "This is not for Mr. Ketchum to know about. He and Stephen had their differences. No, this is between you and me. I want you to find my son's murderer and kill him."

Her words hung heavily in the air.

I started to get up. "Mrs. Ketchum, I really don't think this is for me. I won't mention our conversation to anyone ..." and I started for the door.

"You're damn right you won't," she said quietly. I stopped. "Don't be a fool. I'm offering you the chance to be man again. To redeem yourself. How many chances does a man like you get? You keep walking towards that door. Go ahead. When you reach that handle, I want to hear 'Yes' come out of your mouth, at which point you can finish opening the door and get back in the car with our friend. He will take you home and give you an envelope with $5,000, which is exactly half the amount of the $10,000 I'm paying you. You'll get the rest when you're done. If you say 'No' at the knob, then our friend will take you to a room in the basement where he will have free reign to make as many cuts on you as he likes. Then he will take you, tied, to the Homestead furnace, where he will drop you from a height into one of the furnaces—the one named after me—where your bones will vaporize before you hit the steel."

I was shaking. I knew she could see it. I was afraid of passing out. I could hear the slow hiss of her exhaling smoke and the crack of ice in her glass. If I said yes, I didn't hear myself.

"Start with Alexander Corning, Stephen's roommate," she said. "You can find him in Dowagers Hall, room 125. And Mr. Burns, be polite to people. You'd be surprised how much easier it makes life."

This was how I became a hired killer.

3

From the air, I guess the place would have looked like Eden—lush and green. Maybe depending on how low you flew, you could see the rivers and waterfalls, the brightly-colored birds as they hopped from branch to branch looking for overripe fruit or an unlucky lizard. You might be able to see the fruit hanging heavily from the trees ready for the plucking. You wouldn't have to work if you lived there, you'd think. No farming necessary, just walk out into the jungle and pick a lunch, maybe catch some of the fish teeming in the shallow lagoons for a nice dinner, wash it all down with some ice cold water from the waterfall.

You'd be horribly mistaken of course.

In reality it's the world that Eve and her man were banished to. Strange things slithered, biting things picked at your skin or burrowed inside of you to cause painful diseases, pains so incredible that men begged to be shot rather than to continue lingering that way.

From the air, you'd never know the brambles were so thick that they could maliciously wrap around your legs. That the porous rocks made it possible for the Japs to burrow in like the leeches that stuck to our bodies when we waded through the pools. They set up bunkers drilled right into the rock and were told to never surrender, to fight until death or be killed by their fellow soldiers who were themselves ready to make the ultimate sacrifice. We tried everything—flanking moves, pincer moves, all called by back line officers whose uniforms weren't caked with the salt of their own sweat, whose legs and stomachs weren't cramping from heat exhaustion, whose uniforms weren't covered in the brains of their friends or their own scared piss.

Jungle roots reached up from nowhere to trip us, mud sucked away at our feet, our legs, and if boots were lost, we would die. Period. Foreign curses flew from the jungle all around us. Men panicked, throwing grenades that sometimes bounced back from trees to land in our laps. That night, we dug in and watched rooting logs glow in the night, turning into Japanese signals while birdcalls became whispered enemy secrets.

The next morning, we moved very slowly and at great cost of life through high grass to call in artillery on the enemy's rock encampments. After the bombardment, we moved from rock to rock cleaning out the dying, injured, and still fighting. We, I, shot dying men in the face without the smallest second thought, the blowback covering me in gore and brains that stuck to me and stunk in the heat. After so much death, no one cared anymore if they died. Finally, we made it to an enemy hospital that was also serving as a POW camp. It was on top of a plateau and was filled with the dying; those who we had shot and who had been transported back there. The few doctors who had been working there were dead by the time the artillery stopped. We walked in and methodically, carefully, one by one, we went through and killed every last one of them, some of them delirious, some begging for their lives, and the dead one we put a bullet into anyhow, just for good luck. Two of my closest friends, boys who two days prior had been crying softly on the transport, went to work cutting out tongues and ripping off the pants of the dead to saw off their penises. In their eyes was a wild joy. Another soldier took exaggerated time in unbuttoning his fly, fishing his cock out and pissing a long stream into the gaping mouth of a dead Jap. I didn't know what to do. My body was still flooded with adrenaline, my knees shaky, and a fever raking my head and making my eyes burn. I stalked around, looking for something to claim as my own war prize.

They had tried to make the place a home, building small reed huts for privacy. Some of them had open sides to catch the breezes that now spread the smell of burning flesh; a smell I remembered from hometown pig roasts. Above the huts and near a graveyard, small cloth flags painted with red and black designs, like hastily scribbled signatures, fluttered. Further on, behind the huts, someone had tried to plant a garden, thin orderly rows of seedlings and sprouts, the sort of thing my mother always tried back home. Watering each evening, tying up her hair to root among the plants, crushing aphids and drowning slugs in Duquesne beer pilfered from my father. Her hands grew hard and thorny through the summers. She would pay me a penny a rock that I dug out of her garden. She said that it was the improvement of the soil that interested her the most. For her the joy was the growing, not the produce.

I sat down hard in the middle of the garden. I was done looking for my war booty. The moment I had pulled that trigger, I already had a souvenir; a scar that I would carry around inside of me. A tattoo reading, "Killer," and a realization that here was something I was extremely good at. God help me, what bothered me was not that I was good at what I did. No, what I felt so guilty about was feeling no guilt.

While the guys with the flamethrowers were burning down the shacks with blithe regard for anyone inside, I went from plant to plant and ground my boot heel hard, until the seedlings were mangled and torn and wilting under the hot sun in the poor rocky soil. At night the strong, sweet odor of rotting men stayed in our noses.

Sometimes I drive around town or sit out late smoking cigarettes, with the sweet tobacco smoke curling around my head and drifting off. The eye of the cinder glows like a warning, and the war seems so far away, so unlike me, that I wonder if I didn't dream it all.

4

None of this was anything I would ever talk about. Not to Mary, not to the few friends who dropped by occasionally before the war and then less and less after I got home. Instead, it lived inside of me. Especially since I had been fired. I felt I had done the right thing. Death wasn't uncommon around the mill. Legs were ripped off in rollers and people fell into batches of steel. Their bodies were instantly vaporized. Sometimes crusty outcroppings would be left in the ladles used to move the molten steel from one place to the next. We called them mushroom caps and everyone avoided them. There were dead people inside, bones, and hard-hats. No matter how hot the steel was, certain things were hard to burn up.

When I got back from the Pacific, I found myself waking in the morning with sore jaws from gnashing my teeth all night long. While I was looking for something to do, some way to explode, this kid, a new guy at the mill, died at just the right time. I was tired of going to funerals. Every time somebody got hurt or killed, for weeks all I could think about was the war. I would wake up on fire in the middle of the night whenever tiny sparks grew into a raging blaze, hotter than any slag or molten steel I had worked with.

When the kid hit the hot steel, the moisture in his body spat out sparks as big as a child's fist. He was dead before he knew it. When the foreman came over, he was pale.

"What happened?"

"You stupid son of a bitch," I screamed. "I told you two weeks ago that the catwalk needed rewelding and you didn't listen and now Slivovisc went and fell in."

And I hit him hard in the jaw. The other guys dragged me outside and I never went back, not to work at least. Something went wrong inside. I didn't eat, stopped shaving. Couldn't sleep. All my senses seemed unnatural. I saw glittering auras of body heat around every-one, and they made me sick. I couldn't look in the mirror for fear of seeing their glowing, sparking lights. I couldn't kiss my daughter goodnight for fear of her sparkle.

For a week, I stood outside the mill, alternately watching peo-ple's lights and telling anyone who would listen that the workers were getting screwed over, that the union had deserted us, that the union officials spent too much time on the links and sipping drinks in the Duquesne Club and not enough time on the floor. No one would lis-ten, not the least because I shrunk away from them when they came to talk to me, lest their glow bleed into my body and mark me.

After a week, security showed up and told me to leave. I wouldn't. I was hit with a club in the crotch, and as I was bent over retching, they started working my kidneys. For the next four weeks, I laid in bed while Mary took care of me. My friends, the ones I still had left, now long gone, came round to talk to me, but I didn't want to hear from them. People said they saw my point, that we should do something, start a rival union, or send someone else up, maybe even me, to the election. I didn't care anymore. Three days later when my father-in-law, a shop steward, came by to swear at me and tell me that I had been blacklisted, I rolled over and faced the wall and told him very quietly, but very assuredly to go fuck himself. And as far as I know, he did because I never saw him again.

I stayed in the house during the day. At first, I walked Elizabeth to school, but she asked me to stop. The kids were teasing her at recess about the way I stared and jerked, and about the pint of rye that peeked from my back pocket. Mary went to work six weeks after my riot, and by that time, she was surprised that with my last name she could even get a clerk's job.

And so I stayed at home. Each day was marked by the progression of the sun, its heat smearing across the linoleum tile. Some days I would strip naked and watch the light trace its slow travel, knowing that when it met a certain dirt encrusted crack that it meant that my wife and child would be home soon. But, sometimes, I had trouble fixing their names, or I could remember their names, but when they returned home I was amazed because they weren't who I thought they were, who I wanted them to be, or who they needed to be. They had different faces and different smells, instead of the lovely floral smell I remembered. Now, they smelled as if they didn't really exist or as if they were made of corrugated cardboard that had drawn slightly damp. Sometimes at dinner, my heart would begin to race and I would have to lay down on the floor. My wife and child remained deadly silent at these times, as if they were witnessing a miracle or an act of passion. Once as I lay there, my daughter drew too close and I smelled her dead, flat smell, and she made me sick. I forced down the gorge and then ran to the bathroom, where I dry heaved for an hour.

Finally, about year ago, I felt a quiet nagging. As I lay on the floor, in the late summer sun, naked, I felt that I should match its heat, or at least respond to it. And so, on the 28th of August, my wife came home early from lunch and found me hunched naked in the kitchen struggling with some of her clothes, some of mine, some of my daughter's, my Zippo, and a can of lighter fluid trying to start a fire.

The real reason people fall in love, the one that no one talks about, is the sense of sanctuary. That overwhelming sense of living in a cork-paneled room into which nothing can penetrate.

5

The house echoed with my guilt when I got home at 2:30 in the after-noon. Lizzie would be home in ten minutes. The money felt like a lodestone next to my heart. I took it out and laid it on the kitchen table, along with the day's mail. I took five large out of the envelope, doubled it over, put it in my pants pocket for a minute, then put the money back in the envelope on top of the other letters.

Mary got home at 5:30 and headed for the mail. When she opened the envelope, her eyes swelled. Lizzie milled about the living room, singing to herself as she played Cat's Cradle.

"Where did this come from?"

"I got a job."

"What do you mean you got a job?"

"I'm doing a favor for some people."

"What the hell do you mean? A favor for some people? Is this Mafia money?" We lowered our voices so Lizzie wouldn't hear.

"I don't know." I said. "I don't think so. A guy came and picked me up today and took me to the Kethcums. Her son is dead and she's paying me to find the guy who did it."

"No."

"What do you mean?"

"I mean no. I don't even understand what you're talking about. A man? The Ketchums? You're not making sense again. This is just like the fire last year."

"It's nothing like last year! We need the money."

"Not this money we don't."

"I don't have a choice. I have to do it."

"Why?"

"Because, goddammit."

"But why you? Why you?"

But when she said it, all I heard was her saying, "Why me? Why am I married to a man like this? What did I do to deserve this?"

"It's not up for debate." I said. "We'll take the money. Pay our bills. It's a one-time thing."

"I'm scared. I don't like this."

"Take the money. Pay the bills."

Dinner was a silent affair except for Lizzie chirping about reading and a puppy she had seen on the way home.

"Can we get a dog?" she asked.

"We don't have the money," Mary snapped.

"Maybe," I said. "Maybe we can get a dog."

That night, after Lizzie was in bed, Mary and I made love for the first time in weeks. Our hipbones clashed together, and as she rolled on top of me, as I looked up at her, I could see her aura again. Light shining around her like a halo around the moon. I tensed up, and the warmth of her surrounding me turned ice cold. I rolled her back over and finished quickly, trying to get back into my body, trying to pull myself away from the images of the dead that played inside my head and the rage that knocked around inside of my rib cage. Afterwards she cried, and I felt awkward and empty inside.

"What's going on?" she asked through tears. "Why won't you tell me?"

"I told you everything I know."

"I wish you hadn't. I wish you hadn't done whatever you did to cause this and I wish that you had never told me about it. I wish you had just burnt the money or given it to the nuns."

"But I didn't," I said. "I brought it home and now we can pay everything without asking your parents for money. Isn't that what you wanted?"

The last words were cruel and harsh, and I knew they were a lie. She didn't have anything to do with this, it was all me. But I said them anyhow. After all, hadn't Adam taken Eve with him out of that garden to raise their little family? Maybe that fool marched, maybe he crawled, begging for forgiveness with every inch. Me, I had eaten a goddamn apple down to the core and swallowed the seeds so they could grow inside me.

6

Opportunities are like streetcars. They don't exist in Pittsburgh anymore. But that one early fall Thursday morning, which would have smelled clear and crisp anywhere else, hung dark with the soot of the steel city. And yet, it was full of opportunity. If I could do this one thing, this one act of contrition, everything would be fixed.

When I woke up that morning, Mary and Lizzie were already gone for the day. By ten, I had showered and shaved, gotten dressed and headed off to Oakland to talk to Stephen Ketchum's roommate. see p 68 The small houses here in my neighborhood, Troy Hill, were dotted with new immigrants, all of them headed for work in the mills, a step up from the mines where they would have been, and some still were, twenty or thirty years ago. But in Oakland, Miller Sibley is built on rolling hills far from the stink of the mills—the whole reason the rich moved here in the first place. I parked on the street and set off to find the kid.

The whole place smelled good. My neighborhood smelled smoky and acrid, and it burnt the nose and throat. Here, everything was different. The air was fresh, clean with just a hint of decay from the few fall leaves that escaped through the rakes of the groundskeepers. It was like walking through an invisible barrier. The rich, when they decided to put their kids up here, also made sure that the soot and stink from the mills that bought these kids their bucks and Brooks Brothers jackets wouldn't be here to sully their college experience. It was a beautiful place to be, but it wasn't my place. I was out of my league.

A campus can be disorienting. Everyone bustles with a sense of mission, of self-importance. Even kids relaxing in the sun looked about nervously as if someone knew they were running late. I asked one of these well-scrubbed scions where I could find Dowager's.

Dowager's looked like it belonged on a moor. It was a great grey sandstone building, with an arched hallway that separated a pair of three-story gabled wings. In the middle of the arch were two massive dark oak doors. I chose left, grabbed the ornate handle and pulled it open. I walked in and was faced with a large, florid housemother.

"Good afternoon, sir."

The poor can always recognize each other and know, instinctively, where they do and do not belong. I steeled myself. "Good afternoon ma'am. I'm looking for Alexander Corning."

"May I ask, are you with the police?"

"Not in a manner of speaking."

"Mr. Corning isn't seeing anyone."

"I think he'll want to see me."

"He's not seeing anyone."

"Perhaps you could deliver a message for me, then?"

She stood impatiently as I fished a scrap of paper from my jacket pocket and wrote, *"Mr. Corning. Your life is in danger. The police do not know who killed Stephen. I do. I need to see you as soon as possible. Meet me in front of the Observatory at 2 p.m. -Burns"*

The observatory was the only building I knew on campus. It was one of the smallest, with a copper dome green with age and ivy climbing up its walls. It was a local landmark, although it hadn't been used by the school for years. I had no idea whether the kid would fall for this or not, but I sat on a bench outside the observatory, feeling nervous and full of purpose just like everyone else on this campus. Even the people who I assumed to be professors ran across campus with their tweed rustling, looking for all the world like a lost tribe of crew-cut and horn-rimmed bachelor uncles. A sweatier than average student came up beside me. He was non-descript, in chinos and bucks. He was medium height with sandy colored hair that he ran his hands through as he approached me.

"Burns?"

"Maybe."

"I'm Corning."

"Pleasure, Mr. Corning. Have a seat." I motioned to the space on the bench beside me. He sat down. For the first time in a long time, maybe since the war, I felt like I was in control. I knew I was just play-acting, but Corning didn't and that made all the difference. I offered him a cigarette from a fresh pack of Camels I had bought this morning on my drive over. It felt good to have some pocket money again.

"Not on campus," he looked at me as if I had offered him a whore. "I can't smoke on campus. We're not allowed."

I laughed and lit one, slowly savoring it, "That," I said, "is too goddamned bad."

"Look," he said, "what do you think you're doing with this mysterious note and ..."

"Wendy the Wet Nurse back at your dorm wouldn't let me talk to you. This seemed like the best way."

Some of the students had perfected the thousand-yard glance, a look that bored right through you. They were GI Bill boys I guessed, and I thought about what it would be like to go to college for a moment. These beefy guys, they stuck out like sore thumbs next to the rest of the population, unlike willowy guys like Corning.

"Are you listening?"

"Of course," I lied.

"Well?"

"Look," I said, "I'm going to cut to the chase. I've been hired to find Stephen's killer."

"They already arrested a nigger for it." His sneer suggested he had more to say about it, but I cut him off.

"Yes, yes they did," I ground out the cigarette beneath my foot. "But he didn't do it."

"How do you know?"

"I know things, Alex. That's my job. Just like I know that you know something about Stephen's death that you haven't told anybody yet. Until now. Now you're going to tell me."

"Fuck you. You're crazy."

He started to get up, but I reached over and grabbed the soft spot above his knee and crushed it in my hands as hard as I could.

"AAAAhhhh Jesusss!" he yelped. "What the fuck?"

It's a small thing really. The sort of painful thing that guys do to each other when they're joking around. My old man called it a horse bite. But if you hold on, it deadens the nerves. The pain gets worse and the leg starts to feel like it's going to explode. I leaned close to him and tightened my grip.

"If you fuck with me, you'll wish you ended up like your buddy."

Maybe he didn't know anything. But most likely he did. Something, that because of honor or friendship, he hadn't told the police, or maybe the police weren't thorough enough. Maybe they decided a black guy did it the moment they saw the body. I was going to be thorough.

"Now I said, what was Stevie doing the night he was killed?"

"I don't ... ahhhh ..."

I tightened my grip and ground the cartilage against bone. I was starting to wish that he would shut up. I knew that soon we would attract attention.

"If you don't tell me, I will cripple your leg. You will never walk like a normal man. I, however, will walk away like nothing ever happened and leave you here."

"He was swimming."

I let go.

"What?"

Corning rubbed his knee. "He was swimming. He wasn't supposed to be. The coach, he gave him special permission, had a key made up and everything. He liked Stephen. Everyone did. He was a good guy."

"What's this guy's name? The coach?"

"John. John Packel. He's a hunkie. A big one, with blonde hair and little glasses. He drives a beat-up black Hudson."

"You know an awful lot about him."

"I'm a swimmer too. All of us were. He's our coach"

"You ever go nightswimming? You and Stevie ever go over for a little nightswimming, maybe with a couple of hometown honeys?"

"No, Steve wouldn't ... I mean, I didn't have a key and Stevie was weird about stuff like that. Said he wanted to get his extra practice alone."

"You sure about that?"

"Yes!"

"Where can I find your big hunkie?"

"The field house, I guess." He started to get up. "Can I go now?"

"Sure, run along," I said. He stood up. "And Corning? If I hear that you told anyone about our conversation, I'll rip your nuts off and feed them to you."

After he left, I lit another one of my new cigarettes and watched the Zippo's flame shiver as my hand shook with adrenaline. I had to play the tough guy, pushing everything else to the back of my mind, but what if the kid had hit me in the face? What if I had started to see the sparks that I knew danced around him? What if the cops had shown up? I sat on the bench and watched the people go by, anxiously eyeing each other, and me.

7

When I stopped shaking, I asked another student for directions to the field house. The walks were impeccably maintained, the grass too well-manicured to ever have been stepped on. I wondered where these kids were when I was at war. Five years ago, they'd still be in high school, drinking at beer blasts in Squirrel Hill and Schenely Park, knowing that no matter what happened, their daddies would buy them out of military service. No, kids like this didn't even have to acknowledge the war. Instead, they wondered when Susie Cotton panties would let them go to third base, and what kind of engineering they wanted to study before their father hired them at twice or even three times the salary a puddler like me made.

The field house was huge, arched with dirty windows, and covered with ivy. I hustled around to the parking lot, which was uncharacteristically full of cigarette butts and broken glass. Sure enough, a beat to hell Hudson was parked outside. I did a quick walk-by. The dashboard was sagging. There was a satchel in the back. The seats were starting to crack. Apparently swim coaches didn't get paid too well, even at rich boy schools like Miller Sibley. At the desk inside, I asked for Packel.

"He can't come out; he's in practice right now."

"Oh, he won't mind if I go in," I said. "I'm an old friend."

The clerk smirked. "I'm sure you are, sir. The natatorium is straight ahead, then follow the hall to the right and go through the double doors at the end."

My heels clicked and echoed, but as I made the turn, the noise from the pool was immediately evident. Yells splashed out, a louder voice yelling over top of it all. Packel, I guessed. The natatorium doors were propped open. Inside, it was stuffy and hot, like a greenhouse. Steam lined the skylights and sunbeams cut through to the water. Ten, maybe twelve, boys swam endlessly back and forth, flipping at the end like otters. Their coach, Packel, strutted back and forth, pacing alongside them, above them, screaming at them hunched on his ass from the gutter, yelling encouragement, disparagement, and stroke advice. He was a large man, six feet at least, with broad shoulders and a v-shaped upper body. His glasses sat uneasily on his nose and his hair was cropped so shortly that I could see the sweat glisten on his scalp through transparent blonde hair. When he yelled, his face contorted and got redder. And he looked as if he was having a good time.

"You are worthless!" he screamed. "All of you, not one of you deserves to be on this team." The walls were covered with pennants from rival schools.

The heat lulled me; my adrenaline rush from talking to the kid was gone, and I felt drained and hypnotized and for a moment I forgot that this was the place where Stephen spent his last ugly minutes on earth.

But this was not a place for murder. The heat, the water; it was idyllic, narcotic. I could see how this could lead to suicide, but not homicide. If no one else was around, it would be calming. You could slip into the deep end, take a couple of deep breaths, and that would be it. A lifetime of mistakes, years of screwing up, unanswerable questions, all finished in a few minutes.

The swimmers brought me out of my reverie. They were horsing around on the slippery deck, snapping each other with towels and wrestling. They were young, youthful, and they all looked exactly alike. Packel stayed after they were gone to pick up kickboards and pack his bag. When he started to walk out, he got three steps below me before he noticed me.

I stood up. "Packel?"

He started. "Who are you?"

"I'm a friend of Stephen's."

He smiled. "You're full of shit."

He had a thicker accent when he was screaming. Now his words just seemed dark, and his intonation made everything he said sound incredibly important.

"Can I talk to you for a second?"

"Are you a cop?"

"Not really."

"That's a cop answer."

"I'm not a cop, but I am trying to figure out what happened to Stephen."

"Read the papers then. The cops already found the man who killed Stephen."

"I'm not so sure that's the right guy."

"No? You have a better answer maybe?"

"No, but that's what I'm looking for and if I could talk to you ..."

"I've already talked to the police." He took another step up toward the door.

"I told you, I'm not a cop."

"And I told you I don't have anything to say." He took another step, and we were suddenly standing eye-to-eye. I took a step and stood on the stair in front of him, blocking his way.

"Look, I know you can help me."

"You don't know shit. Get out of my way."

"Just five minutes."

"Get out of my way, or I'll move you."

"Look, Packel, don't try to get tough with me."

With one smooth motion, he dropped the bag in his left hand and brought his fist against my ear so soundly and so powerfully that I crumpled and rolled down four steps to the landing above the pool deck. Maybe he said something as he left, I don't know. My world was roaring in my smashed ear. I reached up and felt blood. At the top of the stairs, Packel turned around and I could only watch his lips move before he shut the door. I hung on to consciousness and stood up. Everything danced dizzily in front of me. I started up the stairs and made it two steps before tunnel vision dropped me to my hands and knees, retching violently. When I finally made it outside and past the clerk's excited looks, the hunkie's Hudson was gone. Blood had already matted from the small cut above my ear where I hit the pool deck. Outside, the early twilight began to set in, and I was ready to go home.

8

By 1946 it was the Post-Gazette

Lizzie and Mary had eaten by the time I got home. Mary paged
through the _Post,_ and Lizzie sat on the floor doing one of her hand-
me-down puzzles, with chipped edges and the backing peeling away
from the cardboard. She had done them so many times, that everything fit together quickly for her. When I got home, I made a beeline
for the bathroom.

"Graeme?" Mary called as I rushed through the living room on
my way.

"Just a second," I said and shut the door.

"Graeme?" she tapped on the door. "Are you sick honey?"

"No, I'll be right out." I took off my jacket and loosened my tie.
My ear was swollen and red, everything I heard still carried a roar, but
the fact that I could still hear anything at all made me consider
myself lucky that he hadn't broken my eardrum. I looked in the mirror. My eyes were bloodshot and the rest of me carried a light covering of soot. The chest of my shirt was filthy and the pits were completely sweated through. I dabbed some cold onto the mat of blood

and hair above my ear. The clump dissolved quickly, so I washed the pink water down the drain and stung the cut shut with a styptic pencil. I took my time washing my face, and when I was sure Mary was gone, I came back out. She was waiting for me in the bedroom.

"Oh my God. What happened?"

"I ran into some trouble."

"It looks like you ran into brick wall."

"Cement floor, actually."

"Your ear ..."

"A gift from an irate Hungarian."

"I saved you some dinner."

"I think I just want some aspirin and a whiskey."

"I wish you wouldn't drink."

"So do I."

I stayed up after everyone had gone to bed, nursing my drinks and watching the sky. There were no stars; it glowed with an unearthly orange from the lights of the mills. Tomorrow, I would visit the hunkie again, but this time forewarned would definitely be forearmed.

Finally, I slept soundly. And dreamed. The ghosts of the Pacific haunted me. I dreamed of descending through unnaturally clear water. The hulking, rusting ships wait there. The bones of my friends float by. I float without breathing. Fish nibble my flesh, and it's all strangely painless. I watch as barnacles dig in and start to flourish on my skin along with limpets. I watch myself melt away and enjoy it.

9

Friday morning dawned and I imagined the neighbors making plans for dinner parties and card clubs. But it's a funny thing about being unemployed, the weekends are no longer special. The days bleed into each other, creating a never-ending routine where getting up and going to bed are the only bookends. It was after eleven when I woke up. Decent people were already at work, waiting for their lunch break, finished with their ten minute, union-mandated coffee, and headed for the downhill of their work day. Mine was just beginning.

I made some coffee, and by the time the percolator was bub-bling, my head felt as if it would explode. The cut above my ear had wept blood during the night, staining the pillow and the side of my face. I hoped Lizzie had not tiptoed in to kiss me goodbye before starting school. I couldn't imagine my wife encouraging her to do so; we fought the night before when I didn't come to bed. I hoped this job wouldn't take too much longer. I looked forward to getting my hands on the money and getting us the hell out of here, although I hadn't mentioned it to Mary yet. I couldn't imagine her protesting, though.

Maybe we'd start over in completely new state. California had jobs but seemed too sunny for me. Maybe Boston or the Big Apple itself. Maybe I would go to college on the GI Bill.

Or maybe I was full of shit. Maybe before this job was over I would be killed in an alley. I poured myself some coffee and got ready for my day.

Two hours later, I was driving through Oakland. I cruised by the field house to make sure the beat up Hudson was there. It was, so I parked in a spot at the far end of the lot and walked to a diner off Forbes Avenue to get some lunch. The lunch counter was filled with typical afternoon customers: the retired, the insane, the drunks, and any other garbage of modern life. I joined them. As a kid, I had worked as a busboy in one of these joints. The waitresses hated the counter bums who would sit all day over a nickel cup of coffee talking to their cronies, old men who would flirt with the waitresses and leave them tiny tips while acting like Rockefeller, pinching asses and trying to look down shirt fronts.

When I first got fired, Mary talked about waitressing but I told her that I would rather see Lizzie starve than have her mother sling hash. We fought, but I still think I was right. At least the guys who flirt with shop girls are a little more subtle and have a little more money. When a guy pays a nickel for a cup of Joe, he thinks it entitles him to conversation and maybe a slice of ass. That's the way it is in these shitty places, and I wasn't surprised when the waitress gave me a weary look when I ordered a cup of coffee and a hamburger, rare.

A cop came in and ordered coffee, sitting down on the two stools down from me. His shoulders sagged, and the stool creaked under the weight of his skin which was yellow and hanging from his face in fleshy folds. When the coffee came around, he grinned at the waitress. He was middle aged and fat, the brass buttons straining over his chest. This was no beat cop. He was a desk cop and had given up his streets a long time ago.

"Thanks, honey," he said, patting her on the rear and then glancing around to the rest of us to make sure we had seen. Some guys laughed. I looked at him for a moment too long.

"Problem, mister?"

"No," I muttered and went back to my hamburger.

"Oh, that's too bad," he continued, still staring at me, "because I love to help jagoffs like you with their problems. I like to keep my precinct clean. Ain't that right boys?"

And his cronies laughed, "That's right chief."

In the Pacific, before we made a landing, as we all sat sweating and smoking on the ships, the small noises, the creaks of packs, our musty smell—it brought us together in our unspoken fear. I would spend the nights not sleeping, but imagining women, all the women I had ever seen naked or had wanted to. My wife was always there, but she wasn't alone. Some of my buddies treated themselves to whores in the ports, but they disgusted me, the women and the sailors. The women were no different than the ones I had left in America, but with different colors of skin. That, and their lives were completely destroyed. Their husbands gone or dead, they had now resorted to selling their bodes in return for enough money to buy dinner for her family. Their deflated breasts and pidgin English made my stomach turn.

"Might as well," Billy Pinera had told me in the Philippines. "You might die tomorrow." But I didn't. I didn't buy a port whore, and I didn't die. Billy died though, and maybe I should have too.

When I came back to my wife, I never looked at another woman even though I now felt their power. Women on the street concerned me, their bodies captured my attention, but I didn't care to speak to them or to hear them speak to me. A woman adjusting the stocking seam in a shop window was nothing more than a diversion, a show. I had enough to handle at home.

A group of students slid into a diner booth and started drumming on the table, hollering for the waitresses. She rolled her eyes and walked over to face her humiliation. My meal turned to ash in my mouth. I left money and a decent tip under the plate and walked out. Shifts had already changed along with classes; outside, the campus was quiet. I walked back over to the field house and waited.

10

Around 4:30 p.m., Packel came out and got into his car. I tailed him to his home just out of the Hill neighborhood, a black neighborhood where well-off whites went to hear jazz and taste a little of what they thought was exotic. Packel walked inside his house and closed the door behind him. I parked on the street four houses up and waited.

Instead of the glow that the evenings usually carried, that night the sky fell as black as an exploding light bulb—a bright flash and then darkness. I sat quietly, the chill of fall seeping into my bones brained in through the window which I had rolled down a notch. I pulled my jacket closer; turning on the engine would have been a bad decision I had decided. An idling car at night on a suburban street would draw cops like a fresh hooker. I shivered again, but at least the cold kept me awake, kept me read. ? ready?

An hour and a half after nightfall, cars started streaming down the road. Nice cars. Roadsters and convertibles with college boys with brown bags in their hands jumped out of them and went up to Packel's house in twos and threes. I counted ten boys altogether and recognized three of them from the swim team practice.

I waited another long, cold hour and then slipped out of the car. The house was a low bungalow, one floor with brightly lit windows. I followed the shadows, skirting the bits of light and hugging tight to the building. His shrubs smelled like cat piss and felt like rubbery flesh when they rubbed against my cheek. The sounds of the party seeped through the walls. Loud music and voices slurred, singing along to the music or yelling at each other joyfully as they drank and drank and drank.

I gathered my courage and quickly peeped in the windows. Packel was in the middle of all of it, a big smile on his face, as he poured glasses of Canadian Club and opened bottles of beer. He was sweating again. I was freezing. It didn't look like they would be calling it quits any time soon. I made my way back to the car, and this time the cold didn't keep me awake for long.

I woke with a start as Packel's screen door slammed against the wall and boys started stumbling out. They hopped in their cars with the bravado of being young and wealthy and weaved off. I counted only eight. I waited another fifteen minutes and snuck back to the windows. The living room was empty, with bottles scattered everywhere, collecting in corners and spilt on table tops. The arm of the record player hung at an odd level and one of the boys was passed out on the couch, a stain of vomit on his Arrow shirt front. I crept around the back of the house to the next dimly lit window. Inside, Packel's naked body—its paleness—shocked me. There was a white, almost translucent quality to his skin. His face was blocked by the back of one of the college boys, who slowly took off his shirt and peeled away his trousers and underwear. I turned away. I felt a little queasy. I decided to leave. Packel would have a lot to deal with the next day.

I got home at three in the morning. Mary was asleep, and Lizzie lay crosswise on the bed, smacking her lips as I picked her up and rearranged her in the bed. I put her back under the covers, pulled them up around her neck, then walked into the bathroom, refilled her glass of water and brought it in. I kissed her goodnight. When did it happen, that switch from sweet baby breath to the smell of human decay, the hints that issued from our mouths that while we slept, that our insides were rotten and no good? I reeled back and left the room as colors began to shimmer around her. My head throbbed with pain and I thought for a minute I would faint. Instead, I leaned my back against the wall and let myself slide down until I was sitting on the floor, listening to the wailing in my ears. Even after the war, after everything I had seen and done, that moment, when I leaned over to kiss Lizzie and was shocked at the stink of her breath—that was the moment we all started dying.

11

By the time I woke up on Saturday, the sun was already up and long shadows fell across the bedroom. Mary was gone, but the bed was still dented from the weight of her body. My mouth was sour from the taste of cigarettes and dry with leftover fear. There was no momentary delusion, no question of whether I was asleep or not, no delicious moment of lying in bed with a breeze cooling in from the window, wrapping itself around my bare legs. I hadn't woken up like that for a long time. Instead there was a sudden jerk, my eyes peeling open immediately and my head swiveling from side to side to see who else might be in the room, which was empty. I could hear Lizzie singing downstairs and clanking in the kitchen. When I got there, Mary looked at me appraisingly as I poured myself a cup of coffee.

"You know," I said slowly, "I've been thinking that we haven't done anything fun in a long time. How about we head out to Kennywood today, check out the roller coasters, eat some cotton candy?" Lizzie's eyes lit up, but Mary looked cold.

"It's September, Graeme," she said. "Kennywood's been closed for weeks."

"Well," I said, "what about the Conservatory then? You like flowers."

In the years before the war, we had made constant trips to the Phipps's Conservatory, a great glass greenhouse sprawling across Schenley Park in Oakland. On weekends it was free, and it was about all we could afford.

"I used to like flowers."

I knew what she meant. With her job, she didn't have free time to worry about snapdragons and marigolds and the yard. The gardens had deteriorated until I finally just mowed over everything, unable to distinguish the flowers from the weeds.

"Dammit," I shouted and slammed the cup down, coffee splattering on the sideboard. I'm doing my best here." I stalked off to take a shower before either of them could say anything.

When I came out, Mary was sitting on the bed.

"I'm sorry," she said. "Let's go to the Conservatory."

"Fine," I said, and started to get dressed.

It was, of course, a mistake. To get to the Conservatory, I was forced to drive back up through Oakland, past the college and Packel's place. I started to sweat as the car climbed through Forbes Avenue, even though it was cool outside. Inside the Conservatory, it was unbearably warm, like the field house had been. I loosened my tie and shed my jacket in the artificially tropical air. The displays here were freakish—plants that looked like they came from another planet, lily pads big and strong enough to support a fully grown woman, snaky plants from the desert that sent out arms and tendrils that looked as if they would grab me at any moment. A year ago, the lily pad ponds had alligators in them. When I was young, my dad told me that I could walk right up to the edge of the pond, no wall, no rope and look the gators straight in the eye and the throat. His father, my grandfather, would always threaten to drown the children in the water if they misbehaved. The gators were gone, but the place still carried a dangerous, other-worldly feel. The jungle plants, the smells, the bright orchids dripping down the trunks, the exposed root systems of the old trees—anything could be hiding in there.

Mary ran her hands among the blooms of the orchids when the guard wasn't looking and then played her fingers through her hair, letting Lizzie smell the perfumed locks. How she could stand it was beyond me. The room was already heavily layered in smells, a thick blanket of fruitfulness, of rotting ground, of pollen and honey never to be made, let alone tasted, and of sexually sweet smells designed to trap insects. The smells whirled and charged at my head, confusing me. My breath caught in my throat and I began to get dizzy. Without saying anything, I left the room panting, heading outside to the thick, smoky Pittsburgh air that I was used to. I leaned against the wall, fished a Camel out of my breast pocket, and lit it with trembling fingers. Cigarettes were the closest things I knew to friendship, lately. They woke me up when I was tired, calmed me down when I was nervous, occupied my mind and gave me a habit. Without smokes, I was miserable when everyone else enjoyed them. With them, I realized that they're stealing my wind, and probably slowly killing me.

Before I had even smoked half of it, Mary came outside. Her dress was thin and from the heat of the greenhouse, clung to her curves. Tiny beads of sweat hung in the hollow of her throat and her face was flushed.

"Are you okay?" she asked with real concern.

"Yeah, it was, uh, just a little close in there."

"We can go home," she said. "Maybe this was a bad idea."

"No," I said, grinding out the smoke under my heel. "It's fine. Let's go back in." Lizzie had already moved into the fountain room by the time we found her. Here calm flowers, American flowers, reassuring flowers, bloomed next to a lightly spraying fountain. I sat on a bench while Mary went around telling Lizzie about the flowers. I could have sat there and watched them all day. Mary had a tenderness, not only when she was talking to Lizzie, but an inborn patience when she handled the plants as well, cupping them in her palms to tilt up the blossoms for our daughter to smell or pinching open a snapdragon's throat. We were the only ones inside, and I felt like we were a family, a real family for the first time in years.

By the time we left, the sun was low in the sky, any heat from the Indian summer day had dissipated and Mary slid close to me in the car for heat. Through Oakland again, my heart pounded. My stomach felt loose and slippery, and my hands jerked if they weren't on the wheel, occasionally fluttering as if to brush away an insect. I didn't know how much further I could drive like this. I wanted a drink.

Mary's eyebrows rose when I pulled into a steakhouse for dinner, but the money was burning a hole in my pocket. I had a double rye before I even opened the menu. We ate gigantic meals with a double desert for Lizzie, our first unrestrained meal in months. Back in the car, with the lights on, I felt safe again, content with the meat sitting in my stomach. The warmth of my wife against my side, I had the feeling that inside this small circle of clear light, I was safe. Monsters may lurk outside, but here, inside this tiny sphere where I had gathered my people, everything was all right, that I'd find Stephen's killer, that I was in control and things were not as bad as they seemed.

Home. I sat in our driveway for a moment too long, just long enough to raise Mary's suspicion. I sighed and flicked out the lights, plunging us into darkness. Lizzie stirred as I picked her up, carrying her into bed, putting her nightgown on. She curled around a pillow and we left her with her night light on. There is an elemental fear of the dark, no matter if you're at home or three thousand miles away. I got ready for bed slowly, leaving the light on as long as I could justify, and then, even a little longer than that. Now that we were home, with our daughter in bed, her face softly bathed in a gentle glow, I held Mary tight and realized that the smell of those orchids still lay deep within her hair and threatened to suck the breath from my lungs.

12

I bided my time through the rest of the weekend, playing with Lizzie, talking with Mary. It worked for a while. We ate dinners together, went for walks as a family. But I grew quiet, and eventually my silence was what tipped my hand. The quieter I became, the angrier Mary got. When we sat down in a room together she would look at me hard, and if I didn't answer or even attempt to make small talk, she would stand up abruptly and leave. So I walked warily around the house avoiding her. Finally, Sunday night, Mary wondered aloud, since when did I stay out half the night and not tell her where I was. Her anger might have been stewing in her belly since the night I went to Packel's, but it had been sitting on my shoulders like a heavy, angry, overheated, shitting monkey riding on my shoulder, whispering in my ears, replaying what I had seen on the insides of my closed lids. When Mary started in, I blew up and that devil on my shoulder grinned and dug its paws in tight.

"Did I come home smelling like booze? Or perfume?" I asked, more angrily than I wanted.

"That's not what I'm saying Graeme."

"Could I just get a little goddamn trust in this house? I'm trying to help us all."

"I want to know where you were."

"I was sneaking around the Hill watching a fairy swim coach cornhole one of his boys."

"Jesus, Graeme! What are you talking about? I don't know what the hell is getting into you."

"You don't? Jesus, all of it's getting to me, the no job, the dead kid, the cops, the owners, the fags, everybody dying, that's what's getting to me. The whole goddamn world is getting to me, the whole goddamned world!"

I stomped off and smoked on the porch, watching the glow of the mill from across the river. I knew I was becoming like I was before, when I tried to start the fire. I worried about the same thing. That night, when I finally drifted off to sleep, I was tortured with nightmares. Dreams of Lizzie stripped of her skin and floating just out of my reach, screaming with pain and terror. Dreams of my hands severed at the wrists, with blood shooting out of them, but no one noticing but me. I woke and went back outside to smoke, and I was still awake when Mary dressed Lizzie and they both left for work and school on Monday. I went back to bed with light on my face and slept fitfully until around two in the afternoon. I had to leave before they got home.

I drove around aimlessly for an hour, avoiding my life, my thoughts, before finally giving up and going back home. No one was home, which now seemed strange and threatening. The floor creaked louder than before. I had lost my feel for the details of my home, and I slammed my hip hard into a wall. I sat on a couch for a moment, spots racing before my eyes, my heart pounding. I didn't want to finish what had started. I walked back to the kitchen and poured myself a bourbon. I gulped it and poured myself another to take upstairs.

Our room still smelled like lightly flowered remnants of the perfume that Mary had put on before leaving for work. I opened the drawers of our chipped dresser, sorting through holy cards, rosaries, sweat-yellowed slips until I found what I was looking for—one of Mary's stockings. I tucked it like a handkerchief into my breast pocket and headed back out to the car.

I invented errands for myself that day, buying a loaf of bread and leaving it in the back of the car, purchasing three stamps and asking how much for a year's rental for a P.O. box and how mail was forwarded if someone moved out of the country, but eventually I stopped at the bank and got ten dollars in quarters. I filled one of Mary's stocking with the rolls, double-knotted the stocking, and stashed it in the car under the driver's side seat. I drove over to Schenley Park and sat for awhile, staying until the smells and sounds of other people started to make me sick. I drove down to Smallman Street, parked next to a fruit stand, then cut behind the old cork factory to reach the shoreline of the Allegheny, taking my loaf of bread with me. I took a long walk along the bank and fed the bread to the ducks that skirted rainbows of oil stains to snatch up the crumbs. When night came, I had another hamburger in another diner and, then, when it was good and dark, I drove to Packel's place. This time I parked two blocks away. I stuck the quarter-filled stocking in my pocket, pulled my hat down over my eyes, and walked. Only one light was on this time. I had taken another chance that he would be having a quiet night at home. Sleeping with your drunken charges is one thing, doing it every night is quite another. It had paid off. I was panting with fear by the time I made the door. My hands were shaking and my stomach was so loose I thought I would shit my pants. I took two deep gulps of air, opened his screen door, and pounded on the door louder than I had meant to.

"Yes, yes, I'm coming," he said from inside. Part of me was trying to justify this as finishing Mrs. Ketchum's job, but a bigger part just wanted to beat the shit out of the hunkie for cuffing my ear.

I have a point where my fear turns to rage. My eyes cloud and I become animalistic. Spit shoots from my mouth and drips down my face, my eyes bug and roll. I always wanted to be a Bogart, smooth and collected even when fighting, or at least I expected to have the deadly professionalism of a Rocky Marciano. But I don't. The rage turns into a physical pain between my shoulder blades, and finally, I'm a monster. Sometimes I invite it, making my hate a cozy nest and encouraging it to speak out.

When Packel opened the door, I hit him as hard as I could between the eyes. He stumbled, fell backwards into an end table and then onto the floor. I walked into his house, slammed the door behind me, brought the stocking out of my pocket, and swung it down hard on his face again. His nose cracked like a chicken bone being snapped in half. Blood sprang from between his fingers where he reached up to hold his face. He screamed and I panicked, screaming along with him, swinging again, hitting him in the crotch with all forty quarters and all the elasticity left in Mary's cheap stockings. Packel let out a high-pitched noise and reached for his lap. I swung one last time, hitting him hard in the face again, squarely in the mouth. He screamed again but now the foam that sprang to his lips was flecked with blood. He crumpled to the floor. I kicked him over onto his back with my foot, and stood hard on his throat.

"All right, you fuck, listen to me. Remember me? I'm the one you pushed down the steps, you fucking queen. Remember me?" I stepped off his throat.

He looked up, dazed by the pain. "What do you want?" he asked, his voice raspy and gasping from the pressure of my foot.

"The same goddamn thing I asked for the other day. Some goddamn answers about Ketchum."

"I don't know anything."

I swung the stocking hard, catching him in the balls again. Before he could squeal, I swung again and hit him low in the chest, knocking the air out of him.

"Listen you fucking queen, I know all about your parties. I know you screw your swimmers. Were you fucking Ketchum? Is that what happened? Huh? He made you mad and you killed him? A little love affair gone wrong, a little queer crime of passion?"

"No ..." he panted.

"Don't you fucking lie to me!" I brought the stocking up again and he winced.

"No! No! It wasn't me."

I stopped the downswing.

"Now we're getting somewhere. Who was it?"

"I don't ..."

I wound up hard and dealt him one to the ribs. He was crying now.

"I said, don't you fucking lie to me. I'll beat you until you can't fucking move. I'll fucking cripple you, and the cops will look as hard for your assailant as they did for Ketchum's killer. And I'll write anonymous letters to the parents of every last goddamn member of your swim team and tell them what you did, and then I'll tell the papers. You'll wish I had killed you." The words flew out of me. My sweat and spit shot onto his bloody face. He winced as if it was laced with acid.

"Johnny Silver," he said.

"What?" And I raised the quarters again.

"Johnny Silver. He was Stevie's lover. I introduced them."

"That's sweet. Where can I find this Silver?"

"Check the Global Grill, on the Hill."

"I'll do that Queenie, and so help me, if I don't find him, I'll be back with those letters in my hip pocket."

The old monkey dug its claws into me once again and began howling. Great gobs of color, oranges and greens, flowed around Packel and mixed with the red fog of my eyes and the scarlet of his blood that pooled on his face and under his head. I knelt beside him and looked in his eyes. He looked back at me until his imploring eyes turned to soft fear, and then I started my backswing. I hit him three or four more times in his face with the roll, I saw one of his teeth crack out, and when I stood up I saw myself in the mirror and didn't know who this foam-flecked, blood-splattered man was. Slowly, the monster left me, its job done, searching for greener pastures. I left Packel unconscious on the floor, shut the doors carefully behind me, and vomited my hamburger, rare, all over his lawn.

13

Right after I came home from the war, I had trouble sleeping. I would lie down at night, curling as close as I could to Mary. But when her breathing turned slow and regular and her shoulders dropped the tension of the day, then I would get up and pace the house, drinking coffee, sitting outside if it was a nice night, smoking, and watching the world shut down. At night, everything was resting except for the mills still belching their smoke and fire, and I wondered about the guys humping third shift. When I looked around at the night birds or the opossum skittering from trash can to trash can or the occasional waddling skunk, I was amazed that I had traveled so far, done so much good and so much bad, and that I made it right back where I started. Nothing had changed, I tried telling myself, but the world had a strange new patina, a roughness that made even the softest noise sound like an explosion, and more hurtful than broken promises. When I heard a twig snap from a raccoon family's wanderings, I stiffened. I checked on Lizzie six or eight times a night. When I did mange to fall asleep on the porch or couch, I woke up bathed in sweat, sometimes screaming and swinging. But that was years ago. I'm better now.

I stayed up the rest of the night when I got home from Packel's place. My heart was still racing when I got to our front door. Inside, my family was asleep. I had the uncontrollable feeling that I had gone too far, taken the step over the line. I poured myself a drink and sat on the porch, smoking cigarettes until the third shift came home and Lizzie and Mary left for the day. Tuesday morning, I went back inside and slept.

In my dreams, I was back in the Pacific. We were about to land, but I had no hands. Everyone was rammed into the landing craft, all of us swearing and shuffling, and no matter how loudly I screamed no one would help me. No one would admit that I had no hands and that on hitting the beach, I would be a sitting duck.

A pounding on the door woke me up at two in the afternoon. The sun had warmed my face through the window and my pillow was wet with sweat. I pulled on pants and stumbled out. It was Mrs. Ketchum's goon.

"Do you do anything but sleep, jackass?"

"What do you want?" I asked, no sleep left in my head, suddenly wanting a cigarette.

"I don't want shit pal, Mrs. Ketchum's the one that wants. And she's waiting out in the car." He jerked his thumb and I saw the long black Lincoln parked a ways down the block. "Put on some pants, tough guy, and we'll go see the missus."

Inside, the car was unnaturally cool. Mrs. Ketchum sat smoking a cigarette. She was prettier than I remembered from our first meeting, as if the tragedy of her son's death had reawakened hungers beyond revenge in her.

"My son was buried five days ago, Mr. Burns. The colored man the police arrested hung himself in his cell yesterday."

I started, but tried to play cool. "Really?"

"Yes, really. I think he may have had prompting. My question is, what have you found?" I heard the whisper of silk as she uncrossed and recrossed her legs. I wasn't ready to tell her that her son was a fruit, that I had beaten the living shit out of an immigrant swim coach, and that I was pretty sure that this job might win me nothing.

"I'll be honest, Mrs. Ketchum, I haven't found out much of anything."

"I don't believe you, and I don't like liars. What does Packel have to do with all this?"

She was watching me like a hunter, controlling me like a snake will a bird. I could smell her perfume. It was sweet, thick, like lilies, like a funeral home.

"May I remind you, Mr. Burns, that you are under my hire? You work for me, and only for me. I expect you to tell me the full truth as you find it. I do not want to have to come and see you again."

"Sometimes the truth isn't clear until it's had a day to settle, like water from rusty pipes."

"Save your homespun aphorisms for the mill hands, Mr. Burns. What happened with Packel?"

"I thought he might know something about Stephen ending up in the pool since he spends more time there than anyone else. Things got heated, and we ended up in a fight."

"He looks like a goddamned streetcar hit him."

"Isn't that why you hired me?"

A smile crossed her lips. "And?"

"I don't think he had anything to do with it. If he did, he wasn't telling."

"This will not be a long drawn out affair, Mr. Burns. Today is Tuesday, but I will give you one more week. If you have not found my son's killer by then, you will become disposable. Do you understand me?"

"Yes ma'am."

"Good day then, Mrs. Burns."

I tried not to slam the car door. A week! Christ. It had barely been a week already, and I had nothing to show for it except some new scabs and bruised knuckles. For a moment, I thought about waiting for Mary and Lizzie to come home so I could tell them to gather their stuff. Or maybe I should just drive away. Start over somewhere else. Maybe I could find work away from the steel mills. Maybe go out West. There were oil fields in Oklahoma. In California, the *Post* had said, the opportunities were unlimited. Oranges hung from the trees. All you had to do was pick them.

But I was just kidding myself. Panicking. I knew I had to stay and finish what I started. When I got out of the shower, I barely recognized myself. In six days I had already lost weight and my flesh hung loosely on my face. Dark circles covered my eyes and my skin was pale, making my five o' clock shadow stand out more. I looked sick, like my father before cancer took him, or like the guys on the hospital ship who were addicted to morphine. I got back in the shower, hoping that the water would wash some of the ugly off me.

When Mary and Lizzie came home, I was back on the porch, smoking. I had on my hat to shade my face, but Mary stopped when she came up the porch.

"Are you sick?" she asked. "You look terrible."

I didn't answer.

"Lizzie, go inside and change out of your school clothes." My daughter skipped up the stairs, pausing to give me a kiss on the cheek. I smiled but wondered why she didn't talk much anymore. I hoped it was just a phase.

"What's wrong?" Mary asked.

"Just tired," I said.

"Well," she said sitting beside me and taking my hand in hers, "It's no wonder with the hours you've been keeping, sneaking around. What time did you come in last night?"

"Around three but I couldn't sleep so I came downstairs."

"I know," she said, "the bed was cold without you." She smiled a young girl's smile, full of promises. A smile I hadn't seen for a long time. It took me a minute to realize she looked happy. It had been so long since I had seen her like this. She pulled the cigarette from my hand and took a drag, then threw it in the yard as she fell into my lap. She leaned back, touching my face while I tried to readjust under her weight.

"I miss you." She nuzzled in close and for a moment I thought I smelled lilies on her neck.

"Sorry," I said. But I wasn't. I was just tired, and I wanted to be left alone until this thing was over.

"I didn't say it to be mean," she said.

"Well, then why'd you say it at all?"

She dropped her hand away from my face. "Jesus, Graeme, I'm on your side."

"I hope so," I said. I was filled with the uncontrollable urge to strike out, to hurt her. I felt the space between us begin to shimmer. She took a breath and tried to start over.

"I thought we'd just have sandwiches for dinner. Are you going to be around?"

"Of course I'm going to be around. What the hell kind of question is that? You think you can get rid of me that easy, just because I don't work anymore?"

She looked frightened. "I meant because of your new job Graeme. Because of the odd hours."

"Oh. Yeah. Sandwiches are fine."

Dinner was strained. I tried to spend most of my time talking to Lizzie.

"Did you have a good day at school?"

"Sort of ..."

"Why just sort of?"

"Well, Sally and Alicia were playing together and when I went over to ask if I could play, they told me to mind my own business and then Billy kept running around sticking his tongue out at me and telling everyone I was wacko."

"Tell them if they don't cut it out, I'll snap their necks like a goddamn chicken bone."

Mary looked at me with shocked eyes and Lizzie stiffed a giggle.

"You swore."

"Yeah," I said. "Sorry about that." I wadded my napkin up. "I think I need to take a walk."

"If you wait a minute, we'll come with you. Make it a family walk, like last week," said Mary and she started to stand up.

"No," I said, holding out my hand for them to stop. "I need to clear my head."

"Graeme."

"I'll be fine. I just want to get some air. You and Lizzie stay here, I won't be long." I grabbed my hat and started out the door.

"And Lizzie?"

"Yes, Daddy?"

"Don't really tell them that, you know about snapping their necks."

She giggled again as I left the house.

This job. This job was taking over my life. I had to keep things in perspective. It was just a job, like any other job I had worked. I wouldn't have taken it if I had known, but here I was. At least when I was done at the mill, I came home and took a shower and they had only owned me for eight hours a day. But Mrs. Ketchum now owned me twenty-four hours a day, seven days a week, and it was tearing me apart. It was breaking my family apart. And the fear. The confusion. It was war all the time.

14

Outside, away from the dinner table, it was one of those early fall nights where it felt like nature had changed its mind and gone back into summer. I was lost in my thoughts with the last of the sunlight on my face, so I jumped out of my skin when I heard the police siren burp behind me. I whipped around. The cop who struggled out of the car was the same cop who had given me grief in the coffee shop. He unsnapped his revolver so quickly it snagged on the leather.

"If you make a move, I'll blow your goddamn head off."

I raised my hands slowly. He came up behind me and threw me against his hood.

"What the fuck is going ..." He brought the pistol grip down behind my ear, not hard enough to break the skin, but hard enough to bruise.

"Shut up faggot, unless you want to be dead."

He handcuffed me and threw me in the car, my head rebounding off the doorsill. He slid in the front, and the car slipped away from the curve. Mary and Lizzie never heard a thing.

"Jesus, I feel dirty just sitting in the same car as you."

"Likewise, I'm sure."

He slammed on the brakes and without my hands to stop me, my face slammed hard against the metal net.

"One more. Just one more goddamn word out of you and I'll say you pulled a gun on me and forced me to blow off your nuts. Got it?"

"Yeah."

We drove for a good fifteen minutes before the territory looked familiar. Pittsburgh can be like a maze of winding streets and hills that charge up to the sky and then plunge down to the rivers. I always had a mountain on one side of me and a river on the other. We were driving away from my neighborhood, the sloping hills of the South side where our houses barely managed to cling onto the hills. That's what we were called when we were kids, "Slopies," as in, "Those god-damn Slopies are always screaming at each other, all hours of the night" or "Of course the house is cheap; it's a whole damn neighbor-hood of Slopies."

The mills belched below us. We were headed away from the river, away from the Mongahela, towards Oakland and through Schenly Park. We were back in Ketchum's neighborhood. I should have known.

We pulled into the long, looping Ketchum driveway and then pulled around the back. The fat cop pulled me out by my hair and pushed me to the ground, my chin grating against the gravel. I was starting to get very tired of this. I was jerked to my feet by my hand-cuffs and a pain the shot through my chest and back, causing me to wince and bringing tears to my eyes. The cop grinned. Through my tears, colors began to swim in my vision.

"Hurts, don't it?"

Near the back door, a well-dressed man chipped golf balls across the lawn. As he heard us, he turned with a smile.

"Ah, Mr. Burns."

The cop jerked my arms up behind my back again, and I squeaked out a "Yes."

"Yes *sir* to you, punk," said the cop and twisted some more.

"Michael, I don't think anymore of that will be necessary. Right, Mr. Burns?"

"Uh-huh."

Ketchum motioned and the cop uncuffed me, then stood with his hand on his holster.

"Have a seat."

"Prefer to stand, thanks."

Ketchum shrugged. He sat and sipped a drink with a sliver of fresh lime floating it. "Why are you causing me such pain, Mr. Burns?" His pinky ring glowed red in the light, the design seeming to float in the depths of the stone. Ketchum smiled and twisted his hand to catch the light, saying, "You're admiring my ring. I'd wager someone like you has never seen anything like it."

"No," I said my arm still painful from the cop, "but it's the same color as your wife's panties."

A baton slammed into the small of my back and I rolled, screaming, in the gravel. Why had I shot my mouth off like that? This wasn't a battle I could win.

Ketchum kept his cool, even tone. "Why are you sneaking around marginal neighborhoods asking about my son? You're not a policeman."

I had to think quickly. Obviously Mr. Ketchum still didn't know about Mrs. Ketchum's plans. "I want to find out who killed your son. For the good of the community."

Ketchum was bemused. "Mr. Burns, don't you read the papers? They found the unfortunate man who killed my boy. The filth was so guilty, so disgusted by himself, he killed himself in his cell."

"I don't think they found the right guy."

Ketchum laughed out loud, but the smile didn't reach his eyes. "Michael? Michael, did you hear that? Mr. Burns here, a shirker, probably a red, a man who can't even hold down a mill job, believes he's smarter than all of your boys. What do you think of that?"

The club, when hit it me on the back of my head, brought me to my knees, another sharp, fast shock in the ribs brought me to the ground.

"You know," said Ketchum, "I think I agree with you, Michael." Ketchum grabbed a fistful of my hair. "I don't know what your game is Burns, but stay the fuck out of my business. Do you understand? I'd hate to lose my temper with you. Take him home Michael."

To his credit, the fat cop didn't kill me. Nor did he break any of my bones. He slowly, with an exaggerated caution, drove me out of Ketchum's neighborhood. I was pretty sure he would blow my brains out when we left the streets lined with mansions. Instead, we wound up at a slag heap about five miles from my home.

Outside the car, he unlocked the handcuffs. "Give me your shoes," he said, and I did it without question. Then he gave me a smack with the club across the back of my knees. I fell and the slag ground into my kneecaps. I waited to feel the cool steel of his revolver against my neck, but it never came. I heard the slam of his door and sat there for a moment. I considered my good luck as I watched the slag cars pour their big pieces of half melted, half solid slag down the hill. First it was a cool black, but as it rolled its fiery red molten interior broke through and ran down the slope. The heat waves licked my face and I worried that I was about to be consumed.

The sun set as I hobbled home, head on fire, each breath a misery on my bruised ribs, blood from my grated chin dripping down my shirtfront. When I got home at midnight, Mary didn't ask any questions. I went to work with washcloth, styptic pencil, and scotch and realized that if I didn't get this settled quickly, I would be as dead as Stephen Ketchum, only maybe in a more unpleasant way.

15

One week left. Wednesday afternoon, I napped fitfully and nursed my wounds. I pretended to be napping when Lizzie and Mary came home, and Mary didn't come up to see me when she heard me up and moving around eight. Didn't say a word as I kissed her on the cheek and made my way out of the door at nine.

That night I drove up to the Hill neighborhood to find Johnny Silver. I headed back, away from Centre Avenue and Wylie, skipped the nice places like the Crawford and the Hurricane—jazz joints that brought in the big names but were still hanging on by the skin of their teeth—and headed for the alleys that smelled like piss.

Before the war, the Hill had been a glorious place. Jazz guys playing fresh from the Savoy were common. It was a nice neighborhood with a few Italians and Jews left from an earlier time. Before the war, you could take your girl out to the Crawford for a night of drinks and dancing—unless you were black, but no one ever talked about that.

Now, things were different. There were more empty buildings

than not, and everyone who came back from the war with a habit knew that this was the place to come to get fix. It had become a lawless place, and the higher-ups had taken notice. The mayor and his cronies started talking about "urban renewal." Pretty much everyone understood the code.

The city was having trouble absorbing all us GIs who came back looking for a place to raise a family. In the eyes of the city fathers, the Hill was good real estate going to waste. Like the joke in town went, when the mayor said Urban Renewal, he meant Negro Removal.

I fit in among these low-rent bars; my sallow complexion, the smell of pain and fear all around me, the desperate way I tried to make the people around me believe that everything was okay and proceeding according to plan. I fit in perfectly with the fags who couldn't be who they wanted, the morphine shooters who were looking to forget who they were, and the Negroes who had no choice in who they were. The whites who came here were looking for a taste of the exotic, especially in the seedier places. In nicer places, like the Crawford, well-dressed whites brought their wives or mistresses to hear the new bop sound and to feel the erotic, forbidden thrill of being surrounded by blacks. Tonight though, I was looking decidedly down-scale.

The Global Grill was a real hole-in-the-wall, with a wavy glass block front, the only small window filled with a neon Duquesne Pilsner sign. In my head, it flickered, *I don't want to go in. I don't want to go in. I don't want to go in. It's late, I'm tired, I should be home.*

Somehow, it was even darker inside than the night sky outside. There was music and smoke and lamps with red shades. No one turned to see who I was. At the bar, I asked for a Duquesne Pilsner and when the barman came back, I flipped him a whole buck tip.

"Don't think I've seen you here before," he said.

"No, I'm new in town but one of my friends told me try this place."

"Oh yeah, who's that?"

"Guy by the name of Packel."

His face opened up. "Oh sure. Say, how's he doing?"

"Okay," I said. "There was a nasty fall down those pool steps at the college, and he ended up getting himself all beat up." I took a sip of my beer. My hands were shaking and I was terrified the barman would notice the jerking of the beer or the waver in my voice.

"I guess those steps get slippery with all that water."

"Hey, he told me to look up one of his friends here. Johnny Silver."

"Oh yeah sure, that's Johnny in the back booth there." He motioned towards the back and there was my boy. His hair was platinum blonde, and he was a swish all right. More than that, he was black. He might have been high yellow, but he was still black. I drank my beer, ordered another one, and then went up to his booth.

"Johnny!" I said, feigning delight.

"Do I know you?"

"Sure you do, I'm Packel's friend."

"Who are you?"

"Graeme Burns," my mind choked. Why did I give him my real name? "Don't tell me Packel's never said anything about me?"

"No, he hasn't."

"Oh, I can't believe that!" I turned to the guy sitting opposite Silver. "Would you excuse us for a minute? I need to talk to Johnny alone. Personal business you see." The guy looked at Johnny who shook his head yes.

I slid into the booth beside Johnny and whispered in his ear. "Come outside with me or I'll blow your fucking brains out right here." I didn't even have my gun with me.

Silver smirked, but then saw the fear and hardness in my eyes, and his face tightened and he looked confused.

"I mean it, motherfucker. I'll do it."

He got up. I walked behind him.

"We'll be right back," I waved to the barman. Outside, we walked into the alleyway. Silver looked more resigned than scared. He was more than a little drunk.

"Let me guess," said Silver outside. "Another rough trade vice cop looking for a little queer action tonight or he's going to bust the bar?"

I pushed him hard against the brick wall. "Guess again, pretty boy. What do you know about Stephen Ketchum?"

"I know he needs to come over and pick up his stuff, and I know I don't ever want to see that white boy fag again."

"Lucky you. He's dead."

Silver looked like I had hit him again.

"What?"

Now it was my turn to be confused; Silver looked honestly shocked.

"He's dead. They found him dead last week."

"Oh my god, oh my god, oh my god."

"How could you not know?" Was this bullshit or not? I couldn't get an angle on this guy. I started to get scared again. This was not how it was supposed to shake out. I rolled my shoulders, and wiped my free hand on my pants. It left a wet mark.

"I didn't know. I haven't seen him since we broke up."

"Wait a fucking minute. You were girlfriends?"

He was sniffling, wiping his nose with his hand, but he met my eyes. The guy had balls, I'll give him that. "He was the one who broke it off. Said his father found out. His father was going to cut off his allowance, and he'd have to leave school. Imagine that? A guy like old man Ketchum finding out not only that his little boy was a queer, but that he was in love with a nigger as well. His father said he had to have a real man for a son and he was going to either make him a real man ..." he looked at the ground, "... or kill him. Steve's dad came over drunk and screaming. Smashed two of my windows with a big piece of steel."

I remembered Mrs. Ketchum's words the first time we had met. "Rebar?"

"Huh?"

"Was that big piece of steel a piece of rebar? You know, the rods they use at a construction site to reinforce concrete."

"I guess so. I don't know. I'm not one for hanging out at construction sites. Not my kink. All I know was that it was skinny rod, definitely metal, and he used it to wreck my windows and took a chunk out of the door. When Steve answered the door his father hit him right across the face with the bar and opened a big bloody gash right above his eye. Steve fell down and his daddy dragged him out of there. Said he was taking him home. Two days later I get a letter from Steve, breaking everything off. Said he was "changed," not queer anymore. I didn't buy it. I've known Steve since he was an teenaged kid coming in here playing rough trade like you. That letter didn't sound like him."

The door to the Global opened and someone walked out. Both of us stayed quiet. Inside, a woman warbled out a tired Bessie Smith imitation, *I got me a nightmare man. I see him late at night, but he's gone after the cock done crow.* A couple laughed as they passed the mouth of the alley. We watched them pass by, then kept talking.

"What kind of stuff did he leave at your house?"

"Clothes, some mail, school books."

"Let's go."

"Where?"

"To your house. I want to see this stuff."

We walked to the end of the alley, where the door opened again. *Give me a pig foot and a bottle of beer*, sang the women inside, *give me a reefer and a gang of gin.*

Johnny Silver lived just a couple of blocks away, in a nicer house than me. It was two stories and everything was meticulously kept. The lawn was well trimmed, the vases filled with cornflowers, the family photos in a line on a library table. It felt like a home, even with the vacant lot across the street and the hustlers playing the corner. It had been his parents, he said. He moved absentmindedly around the house like a dead man, flicking on lights, motioning for me to sit on the couch. Silver was crushed by the death of Ketchum, and I was so uncomfortable I wanted to crawl out of my skin.

"Here," Silver broke the long silence. "Here's his stuff."

It all looked like crap to me. A blue blazer, a pair of gray flannel pants, some books, Whitman and Nietzsche, and a shoebox full of mail. I picked it up.

"That's his mail," Silver said. "It's private."

"Nothing's private when you're dead," I said, paging through it. Bills, a letter from his sister in Boston, and an envelope that was strangely heavy. It had been opened once and then resealed.

"What's this?" I asked.

"That's what caused the fight. His father gave it to him when he said he was going to make a man out of him. It's some sort of invitation to his father's social club."

I tore it open to find an engraved card on heavy metal, sheet steel maybe. It read:

THE GENTLEMEN'S PICNIC AND SWIMMING SOCIETY

9:00 PM

SEPTEMBER 23

BUTLER FAIRGROUNDS

ADMITTANCE BY INVITATION ONLY

There was a design at the bottom. It looked like a flower from one angle and skull from another. It played in the back of my mind; I had seen it before, but couldn't place where. September 23 was three days from today. Butler was a small town twenty miles north of the city. Ketchum had a mill there too. It looked like I had a trip to make.

I gathered the rest of the mail and stuffed it in my pocket.

"Hey," Silver said. "Could I keep the letter, the last letter?"

I took the mail out of my pocket. Silver looked heartbroken. I sorted through them and picked out the invitation.

"Keep it all," I said. "You deserve something."

I left so quickly I didn't see the car that sat outside Silver's house or the one that followed me home.

16

Thursday. Six days before Mrs. Ketchum's goon came by to teach me the high wire routine. That night I did everything right. I stopped at the market and bought ground round. I clumped around in the kitchen, dropping pots, scalding my hands on boiling milk, and dousing myself and the floor liberally with flour. In the best of times I was no cook, making my own meals only as a last resort. And today, every time there was a sharp noise, a falling pan, or a slamming cupboard door, I jumped. My depth perception was off. I couldn't pour things straight, I grabbed pans when I knew that they were hot. At one point I had to sit down because my knees were shaking, as if I had just climbed a ladder to a church's steeple. When Mary and Lizzie came home, I had calmed myself down with several glasses of scotch and the constant thought that, one way or another, all of this would be over soon. The whole house smelled of scalloped potatoes and meat-loaf, but I wasn't hungry.

"What's this?" Mary asked.

"I wasn't too busy today, so I thought I'd try to make dinner."

She looked skeptical. "Will we die from eating it?" She smiled.

"I don't think so. I used a recipe from one of your books."

"Well," she said, still smiling, "it looks great. Let me tell Lizzie to wash up and we'll eat early."

By six, everything was eaten, the dishes were washed, and we sat around listening to the radio. Baby Snooks was fussing about something or another. I couldn't focus. Finally, during a commercial, I rubbed my hands together and spoke.

"I won't be here on Friday."

"Why?"

"For the job."

Her face fell. "Is that what all this was about?"

"No."

"Just once, couldn't you do something nice because you wanted to, not to soften the blow of more bad news?"

Lizzie was looking at us. I started to get angry. Working hard to keep it together, I said, "Look, I'm almost done. This should be one of the last times."

"It better be, Graeme."

"What's that mean?"

"You're not stupid. Figure it out."

We looked at each other for a long time without speaking. Finally, she clicked off the radio and turned to Lizzie, "C'mon honey, you need to get a bath."

I laid down on the couch after they went upstairs. I struggled against sleep, my thoughts about Mr. Ketchum and Johnny Silver refusing to slow down. Ideas that made no sense were running into each other and bonding. Finding all this information had been so simple, so how could the cops not have figured it out? The answer that I was afraid of, that I was being set up, that Mrs. Ketchum was a devil, filled the back of my throat with bile and I had to fight to keep from vomiting. But why even bother with me? I was a nobody. I found myself grinding my teeth, completely lucid even though I knew I was asleep when I tried to move my arms and couldn't. Then dark. Then a ringing. It was late at night, a little after midnight, when I opened my eyes. I was surrounded by that peculiar thick blackness that the streetlights through my windows did nothing to illuminate. My heart was pounding and my head was full of wool. The phone was ringing.

"Hello," I said, my throat full of gravel.

"How's your fag friend now?"

"What?"

"You should be more careful."

"Who the hell is this?"

"Ask your girlfriend."

And the line went blank. My teeth went back to grinding, my stomach back to roiling, but fear had cleared my head. Being contacted and threatened while my family was at home changed everything. Did Mrs. Ketchum have one of her goons call me? I went upstairs to the bathroom, took a long piss, stripped to the waist, and gave myself a whore's bath at the sink, splashing icy water around my face and under my arms.

I got dressed, tightened my tie, and threw on my jacket on the way out. I'd play the game. I'd go check on Johnny Silver.

Two visits in less than a week. I was starting to be a regular at the Global Grill. Silver was nowhere to be seen. I asked the barman for a bourbon and drank half of it right off.

"Seen Silver?" I asked.

"Not since the last time you were in here." I finished my drink.

"Want me to tell him that you're looking for him?"

"Nah, that's okay."

It was probably nothing. Maybe Silver had the flu, or maybe he just hadn't been thirsty. Or maybe I had just landed in bigger problems than I had previously believed. I considered all the possibilities on the drive to Silver's house and none of them made any sense. Why would Mrs. Ketchum's guys be leaning on me? We've already agreed on a deadline for all this.

The way to Silver's home had been a short enough walk the first night I met him, but today the drive seemed longer. Finally, my headlights played off the front of Sliver's house. The door hung loosely, closed but just barely, askew on its hinges. A window was broken. No lights were on inside. I wished I had brought my gun, or at least my homemade stocking blackjack. I took a breath and knocked on the door. It swung open freely, loosely, with just the force of my knuckles.

"Silver?" I called in the darkness. "Silver, are you in here?" I stood and listened. The house was amazingly quiet. The ordinary street noise from outside—cars going past, the buzz of streetlights— none of it penetrated. It was as quiet as the caves in which we had taken shelter from the enemy's mortars, where a chill settles in your bones, and won't leave even after going back into the tropical heat. My mouth was completely dry. Outside, for minutes at a time, in the middle of the city, in the middle of the night, no cars went by, as if humanity was avoiding this place, as if it had disappeared off the face of the earth, or as if it was a pile of shit on the table at one of the Ketchum's dinner parties. Only the streetlights played in through the windows, softly illuminating the mess inside. Papers were everywhere, and furniture was overturned. Someone had done a number one job on the place. The loudest sound was the noise of my breath and my heartbeat, both ragged and fast. Finally I heard an answering wheeze, a counterpoint to my own fearful breaths.

"Johnny?" I started walking toward the living room. The couch was tipped over. It was lighter in here, with more windows. The breathing was getting louder, but the room looked empty. With my foot, I tipped back the sofa. It fell onto its back and revealed Silver. He was a mess, and naked. His hands and feet were tied, and his face was caked with mud. The floor was stained with his piss. A cut was open over his eye and blood had caked one of them shut. The other was swollen shut. A sock was jammed in his mouth. I reached down and pulled it out. Silver coughed and then retched.

"Water," he croaked. I quick-stepped out to his kitchen, dodging the mess, finding a cup that hadn't been smashed, and filled it from the faucet. When I took it back to him, he tried to drink it greedily, just like the gut-shot men I had seen who chose between dying slow and thirsty or quick and satiated. I pulled it back and just gave him little at a time.

"It's okay pal. You're ok."

"Packel ..."

"Packel did this?"

But he was shaking his head. "No. Packel," he said, "is dead."

Now it was my turn to feel as if the wind had been knocked out of me. I hadn't meant to kill Packel. I only meant to scare him. I wanted to pay him back for beating the shit out of me. But, Jesus, I had killed him. I was in big trouble, the kind you don't fight or talk your way out of.

"Dead? I didn't mean to ..." Again Silver shook his head.

"Wasn't you."

"Who then?"

He was trying to push himself up on his arms and failing miserably. I raced back and tipped the couch back onto its legs. I picked him up and put him on the couch. He couldn't have weighed more than 100 pounds. He winced when I lifted him.

"Two guys brought him here. Beat him. Me. Took him ..." I couldn't be sure if Silver knew what he was talking about. His matted eye cracked open and rolled like a cow before it's slaughtered.

"Took him ... slag heap ... took him ..." and with that, Silver's eye rolled widely again and then closed. He was barely alive. I thought about calling a doctor, but how would I explain it? I couldn't imagine the cops caring. From what Silver had said about homo vice cops looking for a little chicken on the side, I had to assume that he had run-ins with the cops before. I decided to leave him. I would get a doctor who I could trust to come over, even though the only doctor I knew was the old rheumy-eyed guy who had set Elizabeth's wrist when she broke it. Playing nursemaid would steal valuable time from the deadline Mrs. Ketchum had set for me. If I could just keep my hands over all the holes that had sprung in the dam of my life, everyone could get out safe before the flood. One thing at a time. The details would take care of themselves. But first, I had to rescue Packel from a slag heap.

17

Cops, crooks, and military men—we're all creatures of habit, so the first place I started was the Nine-Mile slag heap where the fat cop had left me the last time I ran into him. The dumping wheel on a slag car is shaped like a ship's rudder, about four feet across. It's like a vision of hell, a less sophisticated version of the puddler machines. When they're turned, the car rises and dumps the molten slag. Slag is junk, waste, the impurities burned out of the ore during the smelting process. Then it cools, forming mountains that soar into the distant heights above the trees. Route 51 ran so close to this heap that if traffic backed up while the slag was being poured, the heat would blister and crack paint jobs, and sometimes drivers would get what looked like sunburns on their faces. I wasn't there more than ten minutes before I started to feel my own skin tighten. Ten minutes more, and I found Packel tied to a ladle wheel near a field of mushrooms, the slag that keeps the shape of the pots that dump them, the slag that most of us believed had the remains of dead steelworkers inside. It was a forest of dirty metal, with shards of slag on the ground so sharp it would slice your feet open in dress shoes. On the sides of the lot, pools of fetid brown water trickled off into the ground and recollected on depressions in the slag.

Packel was dead when I found him. In my heart, I knew that he would be. He had been tied there for a while, at least through one round of slag dumping. His skin had blistered and was peeling off his face. Most of his clothes had been singed off, and his eyes had long since dissolved. He was tied with his arms spread as if he had been trying to embrace the great rolling piles of molten slag. His feet had been completely burnt away, not even bone remaining. When I vomited, it sizzled on the slag, hard on the outside but still molten and raging with a fire underneath. His chest bore a bloody mark where the killers had carved him up before he was dead, while he was tied there, waiting, screaming, probably pissing himself with the fear, offering them anything to let him go. While he hung there crying, they cut a symbol into him. From one angle it looked like a flower, from another, a skull.

18

Friday. Five days left. It was dawn when I got home. Even with the bedroom door closed I could hear Lizzie and Mary talking quietly in my daughter's room, getting ready for school and work. From my closet, I dug out the invitation that I had taken from Silver's house after our first meeting. What connected all of this madness so far was the symbol, the rose and skull that was all over this job. I copied the design on a slip of paper as best I could, then hid the invitation in the closet, behind a can of Zippo lighter fluid. I sat on the bed and stared at my drawing. I was at a loss. This sort of legwork was outside of my league. When push came to shove, the only thing I was good at was breaking things.

"Mary?" I called through the door.

"What?" Her voice was cold and flat.

"Can you come here for a minute?"

"Can I come too Daddy?" Lizzie called.

"Sure."

When they came in, I held out the slip with the emblem on it.

"Mary, have you ever seen anything like this?"

"It's not a very good drawing."

"I realize that, I was working quickly. Have you ever seen it before?"

"No. I don't think so. What is it, Masonic?"

"I don't know." I said with more than a touch of impatience in my voice, "That's what I'm tying to find out. Is there anyone at your work who might know?

"Graeme, the last thing I'm going to do is go to work waving a piece of paper with my husband's drawing on it asking people if they've ever anything like it. You know you already have a reputation ..."

"Ok, fine, but do you know anyone I could ask who might know?"

"The librarian." Lizzie piped in.

"What?" I asked.

"The librarian. When there's something you don't know, the librarian will tell you."

Mary shrugged her shoulders and walked out, followed by Lizzie.

I decided to try the library at Carnegie Mellon. It was big. I had seen it on my first visit, so I knew where it was. Plus, Ketchum had been a student there and if worse came to worse, I could pretend to be just another GI Bill student.

I hadn't been near a library since I had been a boy, and the sheer size of the building with its heavy door and cool, quiet interior did nothing to put me at ease. The place was too much like a morgue.

A short, pretty woman with red hair in a tight knot was working the desk. For all her good looks, she was bored. Whether it was from answering students' research questions or brushing off their passes, I couldn't tell.

"Yes?" she asked after I had stepped up to the desk.

"I'm, ah, I'm doing some research and ..."

"Are you a student?"

"Um, yes."

"Which class is this for? Who's your professor?

"Look," I said, "I'll level with you. I'm on the GI Bill and this is all new to me. I'm trying to find out something about this symbol." I pulled my crude drawing of the emblem out and placed it on the table in front of her. "It's for a class. A history class. And, um, I'm just having a ton of trouble."

"Hmmm," she said, picking it up and turning it. "Who's the professor?"

"You now, I don't remember. And I forgot the book and other papers at home. Could you, have you ever seen it before?"

"No," She said, putting it back on the table, "but if it's a history class, Dean Davis is in the second floor gallery. He knows everything there is to know about local history. Is this a local history question?"

"I believe it is Miss, yes."

"Well, then, he should be able to help you. Go through the doorway, up the stairs to your left. When you get to the second floor, the gallery is the second door on your left."

"Thanks," I said. I could feel the sweat rolling down my face. I was a lousy liar. As I reached for the door, the librarian called out after me.

"Wait a minute. Come here please."

When I walked back to the desk, I knew she must be able to see the sweat collecting on my lip. I wiped it off. She motioned me in close, and the whispered in my ear. Her breath was hot and moist, and when it connected with my ear, a chill went through me. It was just a small thing, and maybe she didn't mean anything by it, but that clenching that settled in my balls has stayed with me the rest of my life.

In distinct, warm tones she whispered, "Are you sure you want to ask him? He is temperamental. He might light into you for forgetting your prof's name and for not being prepared."

I pulled away from her and shook my head to clear it.

"I'll take my chances," I said.

"Suit yourself," she said, shrugging her shoulders.

The walk up the stairs helped settled my head. On the second floor, the air was even quieter.

Coming through the door to the gallery, I saw a man who I assumed to be the Dean with his back to me.

"Excuse me," I said.

He turned around. "Oh. Hello. Are you delivering the portraits?"

"Ah, no. The librarian sent me upstairs. She said you were up here."

"So I am."

"Well, um, first, let me show you this."

I pulled the sketch out to show him. He looked at it, and then back at me with a puzzled look on his face.

"Ayam?" he asked, extending his hand.

I looked at him. "What?"

The confusion on his face intensified as he dropped his hand. "Oh, uh, nothing. I'm sorry, but I don't really have the time. You can call my office ..." As his words trailed off, he walked toward me, towards the door.

"Wait a minute," I said stepping between him and the door.

"See here." He started.

"No, you see here. What was that? What the hell did you say to me? What did it mean?"

"Nothing ... I ... see here, the police will hear about this."

"The hell they will," I said and pushed him backward. He tripped over his feet and fell on his ass. "You know something. What does this symbol mean?" I put my drawing in his face.

"You're crazy," he said, struggling to get up. My shoe connected with his jaw and his glasses went flying. I moved and stood over him.

"I probably am," I said, "but I've been that way for a while. It's not just you." I pulled his head up by his hair. His mouth had started to bleed.

"I'll see you dead for this," he said, his mouth full of mush.

"You know," I said, letting his head sag and taking step back. "I've been hearing that a lot lately, and it has me thinking ..." I reared back again and kicked him with the point of my shoe as hard as I could into the center of his ear. There was funny crunching noise. "I might like that." He was crumpled now. "I've always enjoyed the quiet."

"Now," I continued, jerking his head up, "I want to know about that emblem and I'm starting to get bored."

"It's us, it's us."

"What do you mean?"

"It's us. Us and our boys."

"What are you talking about?" I drew my hand back to slap his busted ear. The gallery door swung open. It was the pretty librarian.

"Oh my God!" she exclaimed and dropped the books she was carrying. "Dean Davis! What happened?"

"The prof here fell," I said, opening my hand and using it to help him up. The Dean was barely conscious. The librarian raced to his other side and we helped him to a chair.

"You're bleeding!" she yelled.

"Wait here with him," I said, "I'll go get help."

"Oh my god," she said, "I was just bringing up a few books for you two. I thought they might help."

"I'll be right back," I lied. On the way out, my foot hooked the spine of one of the books the librarian dropped and sent it skittering into the hall. As I went past, I glanced at the title. The Hidden Path: Secret Societies.

On the walk home, I realized that what were to be perhaps my last moments on Earth would be lived as party crasher. I had some preparations to make first. I needed to put on my best suit and bring a few party favors.

19

My wife and daughter were home when I got there. I didn't say a word to either of them, but walked straight to the bedroom and shut the door. On the back shelf in the closet, I found the box, even though I hadn't had it out for years. My Colt service sidearm. It was heavier than I had remembered, and the oil still clung to it where I had cleaned it before I put away when I got home from the war. The box of shells sat beside it. The cardboard was still bright.

I filled the clip slowly, the bullets going in rim first, followed by their lead noses. I had twelve shots and one in the pipe. I clicked on the safety with my thumb. The Colt sunk into the comforter when I let it rest on the bed. I shrugged on the shoulder holster and slipped the gun in. There was a bulge under my suit coat, but I was dark outside and someone would have to be pretty close to see the lump.

The feel of the shoulder holster caressed my body, its weight hidden away like a secret desire. I forgot how it made me feel giddy, knowing that I had its incredible power hidden from everyone, ready to spit fire and death at my request. The straps rubbed across my chest and cut through the thin cotton of my shirt, whispering promises as certain as garters on plump, smooth thighs. I left my wife, my daughter, and my house without saying goodbye.

I hadn't shot a single damn thing since the army, and never expected to again. Hunting wasn't my sort of thing. Freezing my ass off in the woods to snipe a white tailed deer that had never done anything to me lacked no appeal whatsoever.

I swung by the dump on the way to the Butler fairgrounds. Great piles of people's lives rose all around me—refrigerators, sinks, the overwhelming stink of a thousand decaying TV dinners still in their foil. It was a disgusting place, a shoe-ruining place, a place whose stench would stick in my hair for a day a least. I didn't care. I poured a dozen shells in my pocket from the box I had taken from home, to go with the thirteen already in the gun. Getting out of my car to wander through the dump, I saw there was blood on my coat. Was it from Johnny? The Dean? I rubbed the stain and brought my fingers up to my nose and realized the metallic hot smell of the slag heap still clung to my hands, invading my privacy. I felt dizzy. I wished that I had stopped to take a shower before I came here. And a drink. A shower and a scotch would have slowed things down, maybe even made it easier to understand what I was looking for, what I was trying to do.

At first, the rats scattered as I took aim at bottles fifteen and twenty feet away. I didn't imagine that I would have to do any shooting tonight, but if push came to shove and I did have to shoot, I figured they'd be too close for me to miss.

The gun kicked in my grip reassuringly, driving my hands up, but the lead missed the bottle entirely. Instead, the bullet smacked into a wet mound of decomposing newspapers, coffee grounds, and juiced oranges behind the Duquesne pilsner bottle. I was shooting down and a little to the left, but once I made the mental adjustment, I hit it every time.

I had always been a good shot. I had even considered applying for sniper duty. For a moment, I wondered if I still had my marksmanship medals. The bottles shattered, with satisfying little bits of glass burying themselves in the ground and the jagged bottoms of the bottles sticking straight up, spinning, or rolling slowly onto their sides.

While I was reloading, big, gray rats—the kind people say eat the faces of babies in the slums where the immigrants live—they started to get brave. When I hit the first one, it flipped ass over teakettle and didn't get back up. I walked over to see its entire spine from neck to shitter ripped out, and there was only a jagged hole where the soft-nosed bullet had expanded before exiting. A .45 is a heavy bullet; a solid body hit had a good chance of killing a man, or at least it would definitely stop him. These rats, tough as they may be, no matter how many Hunkie babies they ate, weren't man-sized. I killed eight more with ten shots and then got back in the car. My hands were shaking again. I reloaded the clip, put one in the pipe, and noticed that the smell of cordite and fear was stronger than the stink of the rest of the day that had soaked through my pores and into my blood. The tension melted from my shoulders and colors shimmered around everything.

20

North on Route 8 leads through rolling hills and tiny towns with a bar, a church, and some sort of factory ties to the steel industry down the way. I passed towns like Saxonburg and Mars, wondering why people lived there, so far from the bustle of downtown, and wondering at the same time if we wouldn't be better off up there, where no one cared what you believed or what people believed about you, or at least they didn't take the chance to start a new set of rumors about me, about us. What if Mary and I were to move up here, so far away from the life we knew in Pittsburgh? I could open a grocery store by the side of the road and sell gasoline. I could pocket money for beer whenever I felt like it. Maybe we could open up a little restaurant attached to it. People always needed food and fuel. We could have a quiet life, and be our own bosses. We could build a little house off in the woods, away from everyone, with a long gravel driveway so that we would hear people coming and know when company was on the way. I took the turn leading around the steel factory, drove through Lucinda, and headed towards the fairground.

I had spent more time at the dump than I had planned. It was nine o'clock already, but I didn't mind coming in a little late. In fact, the later I was, the better. And the more full-swing and raucous the festivities would be. Easier for me to sneak through the dark edges.

Casing the fairgrounds, there was a dull glow off in the distance and big black sedans guarded by big white men blocked the main entrance. I drove about a mile down the road and then pulled off into what had once been a home, but now was just a foundation sunk in the earth. The house had been burned to the ground some time ago. I walked on the road for the first half mile or so and then snuck through the woods, following the hoots and hollers, trying not to step in mud so that I would still look presentable when I got there. I didn't know what I would find. Girls, I imagined. Whores there for the screwing. Liquor and general monkeyshines and horseplay and grab ass and every other dumb thing that the kind of guys who are too rich for the Jaycees still want a part of.

The woods were lit by a harvest moon, a great orange ball hanging just over the horizon, closer and bigger than any moon I've ever seen before or since. It must have been around ten p.m. when I finally crept to the edge of the clearing in the middle of the woods. The party was already in full swing. Gentlemen of all sorts wondered around the perimeter, pissing in the woods, clutching whiskey bottles in their hands. They shouted to each other. Tables had been laid out and they were groaning, piled high with food but being mostly ignored.

There was a wild, high smell about the whole thing, like the big cat's cage at the zoo, a pure animal smell, so strong that at first I found it hard to believe it was coming from this secluded party of men. A scaffolding had been built not thirty feet away from the tables, with a tent behind it and big pile of bonfire wood beside it underneath the crossbar.

I realized what I was looking at and my stomach started to sink. I was scared and I worried that the mere scent of my skin was going to give away the wild fear and arousal that danced in the air all around me. I shouldn't have come here, and I started shaking. I was in the wrong place. I took some deep breaths and did what I had done in combat. I imagined it was all a movie that I was watching. I wasn't really there. I made myself walk onto the set. My whole body started to chill as one man climbed the stairs in front of the scaffolding.

"Gentlemen!" The man yelled as he reached front and center of the stage. Each of his words was distinct with a pause between each one. "Ayam? Are. You. A. Member?"

"YIAAM! Yes I Am A Member!" thundered back the men. They began to shuffle themselves into ranks. The master of ceremonies continued.

"Tonight is a sacred moment. Tonight a new generation of men enters our organization, our brotherhood. Gentlemen, we have been blessed by the Supreme Engineer, but this blessing does not come easily or peacefully."

The men shuffled. A few nodded in agreement, more simply took drinks from their flasks or glasses.

"With great blessing comes sacrifice and responsibility." He nodded to a group of eight men, four older in their fifties and four younger, in their early twenties standing in front of the stands, close to the stairs. A few members from the crowd clapped out of respect.

"These brave men have agreed to hew to our rules and traditions. But there has been a disruption. There are eight where there should be a sacred number of nine."

There was a pause and the men murmured their agreement. Scanning the crowd, I saw James Ketchum. He was wearing a summer suit, oddly out of season. His hat was askew; the hair peeking out from under it was plastered with sweat, his face flushing, and a bottle of rye in his hands. He took a long drink and shivered a little.

"Gentlemen, you have all sworn to uphold our rules as these fearless men are about to, but there are older rules, rules that come to us from our brotherhood's very start in Bavaria." His voice swelled and took on a rousing, oratorical quality. "Rules of blood sacrifice. Blood sacrifice to cleanse the disruption of the nine. Even today, these rules must be followed when there is such an extraordinary circumstance such as this!" He yelled like a preacher at a revival.

"We have been blessed gentlemen, but the blessing cries out for blood." Two men stepped from behind the emcee like security. Both bore armfuls of something wrapped in black velvet.

"Gentlemen ..." The leader nodded to the knot of eight standing at the stairway and motioned them toward himself. The group ascended slowly, then turned to face the crowd, staring out from their line. The two men with the velvet moved to the first couple and unwrapped their packages revealing a knife, big, curved and ornate, covered with engraved symbols, and a gold chalice that glowed in the fire light.

The emcee started to speak again. Gradually a ringing was building in my ears, a terrible noise like the one that comes just before you pass out. His words were growing fainter and fainter and my eyes started to tunnel. Then one by one, the older men picked up the knife, kissed it then drew it across the palm of the initiates, letting the blood drain into the cup, before moving to the next duo.

Finally, one of the security guys bowed to the emcee, handing him the chalice. He held it up for the rapt audience. "As there have always been nine, so there must be."

The boys mouthed words, sweat and spit flew from the emcee, and I couldn't hear a word of it. All around me, the men had wild wolf eyes. They jumped from foot to foot, shrugged their shoulders, and rolled their necks in nervous apprehension. The last thing I heard came from the emcee, who turned suddenly to the crowd and made me feel like he was looking right at me.

"Now," he continued, "bring out the sacrifice."

The crowd went wild, screaming and hollering. Two different security men led a naked black man forward to the scaffolding. It was Jimmy Silver. His face was pulped. It looked like one arm had been dislocated if not broken. He held his head as high as he could. As he walked through the crowd, the men spit and threw punches at him and even while he flinched, he never uttered a word. Silver walked up the stairs of the scaffolding without being dragged.

It was my fault. If I had just sent him to the hospital. If I had called the cops, he would be in jail, but not here. If I had checked on him before I left, maybe I could have saved him. Now he was going to die, and very likely I would be joining him.

"Christopher."

The master of ceremonies handed the first young man in line a folding deer knife, big enough to split a shoulder bone. The security goons grabbed Silver's arms forcing them out on the railing, spreading the fingers.

The boy took a wild hacking swing at Johnny and hit him straight in the back of the hand. Silver's eyes jumped and twitched in pain, but he didn't say a word. Blood streamed and the leader hurried to catch it in his cup.

"Calm down, son," the leader yelled, laughing along with the crowd, who was now yelling words of encouragement to the young man. "Take your time, son," he said in a quieter, more fatherly tone. I stood paralyzed as the boy began sawing off one of Silver's fingers. It took a long time, and when the bone finally broke there was crack that carried all the way to my ears. The boy held up Silver's index finger and the crowd cheered and long drinks were drunk from bottles. When he went back to his place in line, the emcee took the finger, painted long stripes of blood down the boy's face, then wrapped it in a handkerchief and gave it back, placing it in his breast pocket.

I watched it happen three more times. Blood, missed by the chalice, soaked the railing of the scaffolding and dripped onto the crowns of the men's felt hats below. The crowd became more and more wild, swearing and taunting. When all of the members in line had their turn with Silver, the master of ceremonies said, "And so the final sacrifice is made. These boys now become men and, in turn, our brothers."

Two security goons worked together, tying the chain that hung from the crossbar around Silver's neck and chest, connecting all with a hook at the end, the kind used for pulling tree stumps out of yards. Meanwhile, two more security guys splashed gallon after gallon of kerosene on the bonfire. The emcee stepped forward to Silver and slowly carved a skull and rose symbol into his chest and then, on his gesture, the goons lit the fire.

Silver's eyes rolled into his head, but still, he said nothing. The roar from the flames was deafening, building on and finally overcoming the noise of the now applauding audience. But it was all still quieter than the noise in my head. The emcee nodded and the hired muscle pushed Silver from the scaffolding into the flames. The flames licked his legs up to his crotch. He swung back and forth like a pendulum and writhed each time he passed through the flames. Silver's fingerless hands punched uselessly in the air. The members cheered and gathered around the flames.

They poured more kerosene on the fire. The smoke was thick and black and sooty, but Silver never let out a scream. The colors in my head ricocheted off each other. I could hear mortar fire from somewhere in the woods, along with the screams of my buddies and their paranoid gunfire. Everyone else was yelling, throwing rocks at Silver as his flesh cooked from his legs. I reached underneath my jacket and unholstered my gun. The least I could do was put Silver out of his misery. I took five steps out into the clearing, shaking uncontrollably. When the smell of the roasted flesh sweet as pork fat melting over a spit hit me, I vomited violently and fell to my hands and knees. It only took a minute, but when I looked up, three of the party-goers were looking at me, and one of them was Mr. Ketchum's pet cop. I hoped Mr. Ketchum hadn't seen me.

"What the fuck?" he yelled, but before he had the words out, I was up and running back through the forest, falling, tripping over logs, branches whipping my eyes, causing tears and blood to mix and scourge down my face, sobbing out loud not just for the dead boy, but for myself, for my family, for the world. I ran faster than I had ever run before and when I got back to the car, I found that I had pissed my pants.

I balled the jack all the way home, pushing my car to go as fast as it would, running red lights, chain smoking, and only breathing easy when there were no strange cars in my driveway when I got home. It was a little after midnight. I stripped down and took a shower, scrubbing until my skin was red and raw, sobbing as quietly as I could but unable to get the smell of smoke out of my nose. I got dressed again and sat in my living room, waiting for them to come. I sipped scotch and held my .45 in my hand. I must have dozed off around three, half asleep, in a stupor. I was awakened by screeching tires, I jumped to my feet, gun clenched in my hand. There was a thump at the screen and I whipped the front door open, not caring if it was a firebomb. It was a shoebox tied with twine. There was a note connected and I opened it:

A souvenir from our bar-b-que tonight. We'll be in touch.

The message was framed in bloody fingerprints and carried the same smell I had just worked so hard to scrub off. I ripped the top off the box and inside, on a handkerchief, lay a bloody, blistered ear. Out of shock I dropped the box. Then swallowing hard, I picked it up, walked outside and dumped it, box and all, into our trash can. Then I went inside and scrubbed my hands. I sat down in my chair and drank some more scotch. It was sour in my mouth. I got up and scrubbed again until blood seeped from the cuticles, ran down my palms, and smeared across the gun and the glass of the mirror.

21

Saturday. I was still awake when Mary and Lizzie came out for breakfast. No one spoke, except for when, as Mary was leaving, she sad,
"Will you be home for dinner tonight?"

"I don't think so," I said.

She turned to walk away.

"Mary," I said, my voice cracking more than I liked. She looked at
me puzzled.

"I love you, Graeme. I never thought life would be like this. But I
do, I do still love you." And she gathered up Lizzie and walked out.

I stayed inside the house the whole day. No matter how much I
drank, I never felt drunk. Instead, I felt more and more sober. Last
night, the evening seemed like nightmare brought on by too much
booze, but now at noon, having plowed through half a bottle, I was
sure I had ever felt more clear. I checked my gun again and sat it
inside the holster.

It was plain to me now what was going on. I had my road map.
Ketchum's pet policeman kept popping up in all the right places; I'm

sure he delivered Silver to Mr. Ketchum's sick social club. This picnic, Stephen's introduction into the club, would have been the last straw, the final chance for Stephen to make good with his daddy. But with Stephen dead, did Mr. Ketchum know that Silver was to be the guest of honor instead? Maybe. Probably. It worked to eliminate anyone who knew anything about the affair.

So Mr. Ketchum was in on it too. Now, I was the only one left who knew about Stephen and Johnny Silver, and to be honest, I didn't like my chances. I decided it was time to go visit Mrs. Ketchum.

22

I called Mrs. Ketchum. There was a long pause until she came to the phone.

"I was eating dinner," she said.

"I have something important to tell you."

"Go ahead."

"Not over the phone, in person."

"I'll send my driver around to pick you up tomorrow."

"Tonight."

"Mr. Ketchum and I have plans for tonight."

"Cancel them. Send your driver to pick me up in two hours at the Benedum downtown."

"Why there?"

"I'm calling from a pay phone here right now. It has to do with the investigation."

She sounded puzzled, and not ready to indulge me at all. "Mr. Burns."

"There's an unexpected development."

"All right, I'll have a driver there at nine."

At nine, I would already be at Ketchum's, miles away from the Benedum downtown, where her goons would be waiting to pick me up. I wanted as few people at the Ketchum's as possible. If I was right about who killed Stephen, there was going to be an incredible shit storm at the mansion tonight and the fewer players the better.

It was a weekend night, so I assumed the help would have the night off. Her driver was also her bodyguard and this would get him out of the house at least until ten. Hopefully I would be out of there by then. I shrugged my shoulders against the weight of my Colt.

There are some nights when everything is supercharged. The air tingles close against the skin. Nights like these, my life, my past, my future gets thrown to the wayside and I am free to become my true self. At least that's what I believe now.

That night, before I left, I looked in the mirror. I didn't know who I was anymore. After coming home from the Pacific, I would spend hours looking at my hands, at the ridges and the whorls, trying to figure out how they added up to me as a unique person. How could the police see me if they had looked at those patterns? Now I looked at the wrinkles and bruises on my face, trying to place myself. I though of the time when a lush on the street hit me up for a handout. I brushed past him, giving him a little shove with my shoulder and his spindly legs collapsed beneath him. He fell to the gutter hard and started sobbing, holding his wrist where he had landed on it. I turned to laugh at him, but our eyes met. His face had a dreamy quality that stuck in my head. I carried it around for hours, days actually, until I realized that he had been my 7th grade football coach. A man who drove us as if we were all headed to the pros. A man who had worked in the mills alongside my father and my wife's father, and now probably spent his days drinking Vitalis. At the time I didn't understand how a man's life could change so quickly, so dramatically, and I blocked it out of my mind. Like whistling past a graveyard, if I didn't think about him, he didn't exist, his life didn't exist. His changed life didn't exist. Now I wondered who was whistling a tune about me.

I looked like hell. Green and yellow bruises played across my chin where it was still healing from my encounter with Ketchum's driveway. When I breathed in, I winced from cracked ribs. I limped from smashing a toe on the Dean's face. My eyes were bright red, and ringed with deep circles. I looked worse than the junkie I had seen on the hospital ship. I blinked my eyes, lit another cigarette, and walked right out of the door. I was ready for whatever happened tonight as long as when the sun came up it would be over.

I parked about a half mile down from the Ketchum's house and waited. At around 8:15, the long black Lincoln slithered past me, and I hunched down in the seat. The driver didn't give me a second glance. I got out of the car and started to hot foot it up to the house, taking about five minutes. My heart was beating wildly. Everything looked sharp in the moonlight, with no blurry edges. I was flying high on adrenaline. I left my jacket unbuttoned for fast access to my Colt, and I rang the doorbell. I couldn't tell if Mr. Ketchum was sick or frightened when he opened the door, but I recognized the expression from my own mirror.

23

I knew the bastard wasn't scared. Not really. I had seen plenty of scared guys in combat, the look on Packel's face when the first punch hit him, the Dean when his ear cauliflowered, some of the punk kids on the scaffolding at the lynching. That was fear—gut tightening, piss-in-your-pants fear. Ketchum was too rich and too stupid to know real fear. Everything had always been fixed for him, all he had to do was wave some cash and the problem disappeared. Up until this point of course.

"What the hell are you doing here?" he whispered.

"I've come to see the missus. Is she in?"

"Now, wait just a goddamn minute ..."

"Fuck you and fuck your goddamn minutes," I said and I walked in. I could feel rage and wrath settling on my back, digging its talons into my spine and taking over the impulses that were headed to my brain. I was that other person now, the tough one who could kill and hurt and who liked it. I saw through a thick red outline, so that bodies were now empty shells. This time, this meeting, it was me, not

Ketchum, who was the cool invincible one. Nothing could hurt me, or if it could, I didn't care.

"Darling, who is it?" I heard Mrs. Ketchum from a room down the hallway. I followed her voice.

"It's just me sweetie," I said. And when Mr. Ketchum and I walked into the room, I saw not only Mrs. Ketchum, but the Michael, the big cop from the park. In plain clothes, he just looked like just another overweight man—a scary, untrustworthy, fat man.

"This is a surprise," Mrs. Ketchum said looking puzzled. "Won't you sit down Mr. Burns?"

"No, thank you."

"You're early."

"Yes, I decided to drive up myself."

"What the hell is going on?" Mr. Ketchum asked. "You know this man?"

"Of course I do. Don't you?"

Mr. Ketchum looked stunned.

"Of course he does," I said, "and I know all of you, so now it's time to cut to the chase."

The cop made a move toward me. "Sit down," I said, the hatred in my voice coming out and surprising me, clicking through my wall.

"Yes," said Mrs. Ketchum turning to look at him, "sit down." She still felt like she was in control of the situation. "Now Mr. Burns, please tell us why you've come."

She was starting to rattle me. She wasn't acting like a woman who was waiting to hear who the killer of her son was, she sounded like a woman who already knew. I started slowly turning towards Mr. Ketchum.

"Mrs. Ketchum here hired me to find out who killed your son."

114

"Jesus Christ!" The cop shouted in my face "We found the spook who did it. We ... he killed himself in his goddamn cell. End of the story. Are you fucking retarded?"

"Don't you open your goddamn mouth one more time, you understand, cop? I'll tell you what happened. Mr. Ketchum over here decides it's time for his boy to start learning the business. But he finds out young Stephen doesn't give two shits about it. He's not a business type, he's romantic type. Isn't that right, Mrs. Ketchum?"

She nodded yes and started rummaging though her small handbag. I started towards her, afraid she had a gun. She looked up at me and smiled.

"Do you mind if I have a cigarette?" she asked.

I nodded that it was all right. That's where everything, with a small one quarter inch nod of my chin, started turning to shit. I kept talking.

"Not only did he not want to be a business man, in Mr. Ketchum's eyes he didn't even want to be man." Mr. Ketchum looked down at the floor. The cop clenched his fat fists. I started to sweat more than I had in years, since the jungle.

"So Mr. Ketchum here goes nuts, can't believe that not only is his son a queer, but he's a checkerboard fag as well, so he goes out to meet his son with a piece of the company's finest rebar to make his point. He gets good and drunk, smashes a bunch of windows. 'Make a final choice,' he says to sonny boy. 'Be a man and come with me or be a fag and stay here.' And Stevie decided, didn't he Mr. Ketchum? So you grabbed him one day after class, and you and officer O'Fuckstick here, took him out, gave him a iron enema and then killed him, dumping him in the pool so that everyone would trace it back to Packel, the homo who turned him in the first place."

Now Mr. Ketchum looked confused. He was twisting his ring nervously and I finally recognized the emblem that hung inside the stone. Not that it helped me much at this point.

"But then I started poking around, and when the Dean told you about our little get together, you made up your mind. You grabbed you son's lover and volunteered him as the main course at your barbeque. You make me sick."

"Wait, what?" Ketchum looked confused, "I didn't kill my son. What the hell are you talking about?"

"You're so full of shit I can smell it from here. I was at that goddamn lynching."

"We saw you," growled the cop, "I knew I should have killed you. You should have let me kill him," he said to Ketchum.

"I didn't kill my son!"

"You're a goddamned liar!" I shouted back.

"No he's not," said Mrs. Ketchum, calm and cool from her spot by the cigarette box. She turned to light the cigarette from a match and when she turned she had a small gun in her hand. It was a .38, a lady's gun. When she pulled the trigger, there was a loud report that seemed to echo in the room, and a small hole opened in Mr. Ketchum's forehead as he slumped to the floor.

"Mrs. Ketchum!" shouted the cop. "Jesus, what have you done? You'll ruin everything for us!"

"You think?" she asked and pulled the trigger again. Blood spurted from the cop's shoulder.

"Christ!" he yelled. She shot another one off, and this time it caught him in the chest and he jerked backwards. With the third shot, a hole opened his throat and blood started streaming down his chest. Pure, dark red blood, like Johnny Silver's. He gurgled and clawed at his throat, collapsing where the blood pooled like quicksilver on the polished wood floor.

"Jesus," I said, "it was you all along."

"Of course," she said. "Don't be obtuse."

"But why?"

"Because I deserved the company. Plain and simple. I underestimated you Mr. Burns. You're smarter than I thought, and more diligent than I ever believed. I had hoped that you would make yourself more obvious, that you would be easier to pin to my husband as an accomplice. But when it appeared that you might actually find out the truth, or be on your way to do it, I thought this would be the only choice left. Yes, I disliked my son. He was having the business given to him simply because of his, uh, sex."

She smiled. "My husband was ineffectual, in all aspects of his life. His son took after him. He wasn't angry that his son was a queer. After all his grandfather was, so why end the family tradition?"

She took a deep drag from her cigarette, but the barrel of her .38 never wavered from my head.

"No, he was angry that his son had taken a Negro lover. The man was just repulsed by our little brown brothers. Please, you never noticed that our mills are full of hunkies, Pollacks, Irishmen and all the other worker races of the world, but no Negroes? Maybe you're not as bright as I thought. Or maybe you have a blind spot yourself? When I heard about my husband's attack on the Negro's house, I felt this was the time. I brought Michael here," she waved her cigarette in the direction of the dead cop, "into the plan with a variety of incentives, but then I discovered he was playing both ends against the middle. He was going to end up killed either way."

"Michael picked up Stephen one day to bring him to the house, then drove him to of the slag pits, killed him and then brought him back to the campus. Everyone knew that my husband was angry at Packel for introducing Stephen to his little boyfriend, so the set up would be more obvious. In the meantime, I hired you with the hope that you would kill my husband in a struggle once he contacted you. Both murders would be pinned on you, and I would run the company. But then you turned out too smart for my own good as well as your own.

"So now, distraught over your crippling family bankruptcy, you came here to take revenge against those who fired you, I assume? You will be remembered as nothing more than a disgruntled worker, like Frick's anarchist. I'll tell the police that you managed to kill my husband and the policeman here, but then I somehow managed to wrestle the gun from your hand and kill you as well. It's sloppy, and I can't stand sloppy, but then again I don't have much of a choice, do I? And really, who will question a woman who has gone through so many tragedies in such a short amount of time?"

She took a final drag on her cigarette, dropped it to the beautiful wood floor and crushed it with her heel, saying, "I do hope you told your wife where the first half of the money is."

And with that she raised the gun to my face.

The door opening sounded like the gun shot I was waiting for.

"Mrs. Ketchum?" Stosh, her driver, stuck his head in, the door blocking me from his view, and reflexively she turned and fired. I grabbed the heavy silver table lighter and threw it at her as hard as I could, like a grenade. It cracked her on the side of the head and she fell. I grabbed my own gun. The guy still hadn't seen me.

"What the fuck?" he asked and started walking into the room.

"Stop there," I said as the door closed. He froze. "If you turn around I'll fucking kill you." I told him to get on his knees, hands behind his head. He did. Mrs. Ketchum moaned. I walked over and found the heavy lighter on the floor. I stopped behind the driver and brought it down behind his ear. I felt his skull give in, and he crumpled on the floor all muscle control gone.

"Don't you ever do anything but sleep, jackass?" I whispered. I walked over to Mrs. Ketchum. The lighter had opened a short cut on the side of her face. She was starting to come to, her eyes fluttering enough to show only the whites. At arm's length I held the gun, letting it come to a rest at the spot between her eyes, about three feet away. When I pulled the trigger, her whole body jumped, and I knew once more that the echo would never leave my ears.

THE END

Contemporary Press

current titles

Digging the Vein
by Tony O'Neill

Tony O'Neill's astonishing debut is based on his own
experiences as an addict and sideman to acts as
diverse as the Brian Jonestown Massacre, Kenickie,
and Marc Almond. Through the eyes of his
anonymous narrator, see what few tourists ever
will: the needle exchanges, methadone clinics,
short let motels, and scoring spots beneath the
wings of the City Of Angels.
ISBN 0976657910

The Bride of Trash
by Mike Segretto

Good ol' boy Wizzer Whale has fallen deeply in love
with a blood-thirsty monster, and now, the newly-
weds are running for their lives. Their romance is a
raucous and warped homage to the lurid, gory, ultra-
campy, B-monster movies of the 1950s. Seeping with
bad taste, you'll stay awake, gasping and guffawing
long past midnight!
ISBN 0976657902

I, An Actress: The Autobiography of Karen Jamey
as told to Jeffrey Dinsmore

When little Karen Hitler's mother runs off to become
a hobo, she and her father change their names and
move to Los Angeles. Dark, slapstick comedy and
merciless Hollywood clichés rule this hilarious story
of Karen's manic rise to the silver screen—and her
tragic (and largely ignored) fall.

ISBN 0974461490

Danger City
edited by Jess Dukes, Jeffrey Dinsmore,
and Mike Segretto

The thirteen stories in this collection showcase some
of the finest contemporary pulp from across the
land. Bleak tales of payoffs gone wrong, crooked
cops, stone-hearted women, and the undead inhabit
these pages. Once you begin wandering it's shadowy
alleyways, you may find it impossible to leave.

ISBN 0974461482

Dead Rite
by Jim Gilmore

When an unpopular video game mogul is discovered
in a shallow grave, Officer Hicks does things by the
book—until the trail of clues leads straight back to
him! Fast-paced and deadly, this is one man's dark
trip through the riches of sunny Hollywood.

ISBN 0974461474

Fuck literature. www.contemporarypress.com

How to Smash Everyone to Pieces
by Mike Segretto

Flanked with a lethal but supportive crew of misfits, ex-stunt woman and champion wisecracker Mary sets off on a homicidal, cross-country campaign to free the love of her life from the clutches of the law.

ISBN 0974461466

G.O.P. D.O.A.
by Jay Brida

While the city braces for 20,000 Republicans to descend on New York, a Brooklyn political operative named Flanagan uncovers a bizarre plot that could trigger a red, white, black, and blue nightmare.

ISBN 0974461458

Johnny Astronaut
by Rory Carmichael (a/k/a Jeffrey Dinsmore)

In the future, disco is king. Johnny is a hard-boiled, hard-drinking P.I. who is caught between a vindictive ex-wife, a powerful crime boss, and a mysterious book that changes his life forever.

ISBN 0974461431

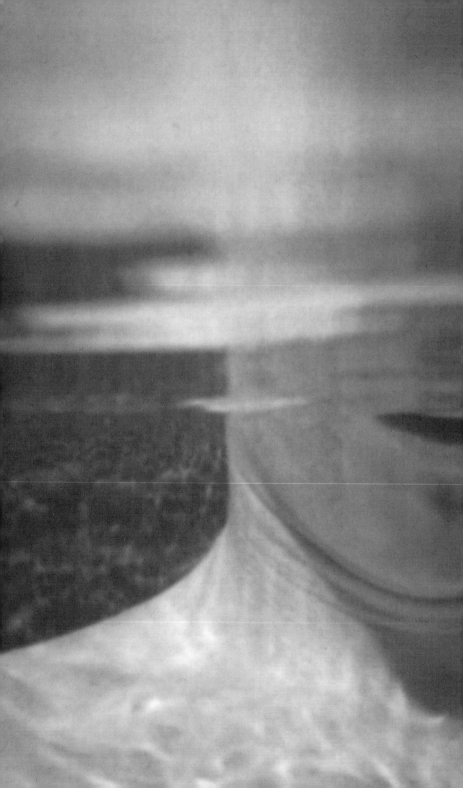